SHAMAN'S DAUGHTER

IN THE BREATHTAKING TRADITION OF *HANTA YO* AND *SACAJAWEA*, THE DEEPLY MOVING STORY OF AN INDIAN TRIBE, AND OF A WOMAN BORN TO PREVAIL IN A LAND THAT WAS RELENTLESSLY SWEEPING AWAY HER SACRED HERITAGE.

"GATHERS POWER . . . SWEEP(S) THE READER ALONG WITH ITS NATURAL RHYTHMS. . . . SUPAYA ENDURES THE ANGUISH OF CULTURES IN CONFLICT, SOMETIMES BLOODY, SOMETIMES BOWED, BUT NEVER BEATEN."
—*The Washington Post*

"PEERLESS IN ITS FIELD."—Dr. Carleton S. Coon, *Peabody Museum, Harvard University*

"TRULY MOVING." —*Los Angeles Times*

"THE READER LINGERS OVER EVERY PAGE. . . . THE BEAUTY AND SPIRIT OF THE AMERICAN INDIAN WAY OF LIFE . . . IS MASTERFULLY DEPICTED." —*The Pittsburgh Press*

D0054784

SHAMAN'S DAUGHTER

NAN F. SALERNO
AND
ROSAMOND M. VANDERBURGH

A DELL BOOK

To all Nishnabeg,
past and present

Published by
Dell Publishing Co., Inc.
1 Dag Hammarskjold Plaza
New York, New York 10017

Dell ® TM 681510, Dell Publishing Co., Inc.

ISBN: 0-440-17863-0

Reprinted by arrangement with Prentice-Hall, Inc.

Printed in the United States of America

First Dell printing—February 1981

CONTENTS

LIST OF CHARACTERS
(approximately in the order of appearance)

Supaya Cedar
Quayo, Supaya's maternal grandmother
Jacques Cedar, Supaya's brother
Jules Cedar, shaman and Supaya's father
Kineu Bruley, Supaya's cousin and husband
Agatha Harris, schoolteacher
Reverend Nathan Harris,
    Agatha's brother and preacher on
    Stone Island Reserve
Aunt Theresa
Neegonas and James, Supaya's sister and brother-in-law
Jess and Kirsten Fallon,
    storekeeper at Two Bluffs Reserve and wife
Mr. Bonnet, storekeeper on Stone Island Reserve
Auntie Em, Quayo's cousin
Cyrus and Miriam Red Sky,
    Wenonga's brother and sister-in-law
Angus Red Sky and Pearline,
    Cyrus' son and daughter-in-law
Maud, Supaya's friend and sister-in-law
Rhea, Jules' second wife
S. M. Jackson, Indian agent on Stone Island Reserve
Wenonga Red Sky, shaman and Cyrus' brother

Hettie and Arthur Bruley,
    Jules' sister and brother-in-law
Keewahd'n, old storyteller
Eli Red Sky, Wenonga's son and Supaya's husband
Reverend and Amy Crowell,
    preacher on Two Bluffs Reserve and wife
Nonen, Wenonga's sister
Marie Able, Eli's girl friend
Jim Able, Eli and Marie's son
Betty, Marie's friend and Eli's girl friend
Soos and George King, Supaya's friends
Sarah King, Soos and George's daughter
Gerald and Lizzie Toomis,
    Indian agent on Two Bluffs Reserve and wife
Mary and John, Nonen's daughter and son-in-law
John and Hattie Bruley, Kineu's uncle and aunt
Wagash Cedar, Supaya's half-brother
Beedaubun,
    old medicine woman on Stone Island Reserve
Alma, one of Nonen's old friends who lays out the dead
Waboose Bruley, Supaya and Kineu's first son
Daniel, boat and coffin builder on Two Bluffs Reserve
Louis Hagerstrom, farmer
Annie Jones, gossip
Harry and Edna Black
Shooskonee Bruley, Supaya and Kineu's daughter
Mrs. Johnston
Caleb Sims, Sarah's husband
Louisa Hagerstrom, Louis Hagerstrom's daughter
James and Ruby, Soos and George's younger children
Victor and Hilda Fallon, Jess' brother and sister-in-law
Marietta and son Eric, Jess' sister and nephew

Frank Jones,
    Supaya's suitor and Annie Jones' brother-in-law
Howard Hadley, Rhea's husband
Josie, Sarah's daughter
Reverend Richards,
    preacher replacing Reverend Crowell on
    Two Bluffs Reserve
Ed Cassety, Shooskonee's boyfriend
Peter, Shooskonee's son
Betty, Waboose's wife
William and Natalie Brent, Indian agent
    replacing Gerald Toomis on
    Two Bluffs Reserve and wife
Tom and Charlie Bruley, Waboose's sons
Maggie and Theresa, Tom's daughters

PROLOGUE 1967,
Two Bluffs Reserve, Ontario

Though it was still summer, Supaya's aging bones felt the night chill. She had made up a fire in the fireplace and had fallen asleep in her rocker. Abruptly she started awake. Someone had whispered her name, touched her on the shoulder. Jess, she thought, with a surge of excitement, maybe it was Jess! Or Kineu. She squinted into the predawn dark filling her house like a pool of deep water. Was that Quayo nodding at her from the opposite chair? Jules standing in the shadow by the hearth? She sat very still and listened. But there was no sound—no knock, no step. Even the fire burned quietly, its embers sending an occasional spark up the chimney.

For weeks past her house had been full of the presences of her dead. She had sensed them about her, serene and comforting, ready to welcome her. Close to her, yet separated as by an invisible veil, they moved parallel with her in a flowing timelessness, their soft voices piercing her heart.

She stirred up the fire, raising a shower of ascending sparks, and reached for another log. As she lifted it, a sudden pain flamed across her chest, shocking in its intensity, bringing her to her knees on the hearth. Her breath choked back, she gripped the rough wood and waited. Slowly the pain lessened and she cautiously raised her head. Her body was damp, her legs trembled. But she knew now that it was time to go. She must not wait any longer.

She took the steps one at a time, grasping the rail and pulling herself along. Reaching the top she nearly collapsed and was momentarily bewildered, thinking herself in the loft of her father's log house on Stone Island. Again she waited, and when her head cleared, she went into her bedroom and opened her old trunk.

Moving as quickly as she dared without rousing a fierce, final pain, she lifted out garments she had not worn since leaving her father's house so many years before. Needing no light, Supaya dressed herself, putting on her long black skirt and the blouse with the quill embroidery on the neck and shoulders. On her feet she put the still supple beaded moccasins Quayo had made for her. Bracing herself on the edge of the trunk, she knelt down and, reaching in with both hands, raised high a necklace. Remembering herself as a child standing before her father as he solemnly placed the necklace around her neck, Supaya lowered it over her head. Lovingly she touched the smooth bear claws and pressed the blue stone pendant to her breast. Closing her eyes, she rocked back and forth, humming softly to herself. But her song broke off when a sharp pain suddenly bent her forward. She must hurry. Reaching into the trunk again, she touched a bundle of hair, hair she had cut from her own head one dreadful day while Soos had silently watched. That she could now leave. She touched a postcard with a torn corner, other cards—Christmas cards from a small English town— and several fragile letters, their smudged and faded words recounting simply what still was cause for sorrow. Those too she could leave.

Then her fingers closed over the cool, smooth surface of a gold pocket watch with chain and fob attached. For one precious second she laid it against her cheek; then, opening her medicine bag, she placed the watch and chain inside. Picking up a delicate bead necklace with a dried-skin amulet, she put that also into the bag. Finally her searching fingers grasped the small stone figure of a sitting bear. Holding it in both hands, Supaya bowed her forehead against it and murmured, "Grandfather, help me, one last time! Help me finish what I must do!" She put the stone bear into the bag, drew the drawstrings tight, and went downstairs.

Going down was easier. She opened wide the front door and looked out toward the east. Ground mist hung low over the field, obscuring the woods. Above, pale stars glistened in the gray dawn sky. The damp air cooled her head and helped steady her. Leaving the door open, she went back through the house to the lean-to. Facing the dark shadow of herself in the mirror, she unpinned her thick gray braid, letting it hang down her back.

Raising her arms made her dizzy with pain, and she leaned against the wash bench until the faintness passed. Gathering her strength, she remembered another morning long ago, another room, dark like this one, the touch of her grandmother's ashy fingers marking her cheeks. But this morning, unlike on that other, she was not afraid. She was not alone. And she knew where she was going.

Opening the back door, she stepped out into the gray dawn.

PART ONE

1897-1901

CHAPTER ONE
Summer, 1897, Stone Island, Ontario

Supaya hesitated on the threshold and glanced back over her shoulder at her grandmother, her motionless figure barely discernible in the dark room. Drawing courage from her resolute silence, Supaya quietly latched the door and paused to look about and listen. The still, predawn air was heavy with dampness, and she drew her grandmother's shawl more closely about her head. Nothing stirred. The whole world seemed lost in deep sleep. Never before had she gone out so early, but she must avoid the eyes of Reverend Harris, and those who would tell him. Two years before, when she was ten, he had seen her going in the first light of sun and had turned her about and scolded her grandmother, saying visions were not to be found by fasting in the woods but by sitting in church. Her grandmother had listened, eyes fixed on a point beyond him, her blank expression masking what she felt for this plump man in black who had turned her elder granddaughter, Neegonas, away from the ways of her people. Since then Supaya had risen well before dawn to kneel before her grandmother and have her cheeks marked with charcoal from the cold fire. Each time she had stayed on the hill longer, waiting to be blessed by a vision, but each time she had returned empty. This morning her grandmother's hands had gripped her shoulders. She had put her face close to Supaya's, her old eyes shiny in the dark. "This time," she whispered, "this time you will be blessed." Then she had leaned back in her chair and closed her eyes.

Supaya moved swiftly away from the log house into the woods that stretched unbroken for miles to the north of the island. She followed no path, only her own sense of direction and feel for the land where she had lived all her life. Often she had gone through the woods and climbed the steep, rocky slope that rose high above the trees to the little pocket among the boulders, her own secret place, where, hidden from view, she could gaze up at the vast sky and at the most distant rim of the world where lake and sky met. She had never spoken of it to anyone, not even to Kineu. Under the trees, darkness was almost a solid through which she pushed her way, bent forward, eyes straining to pierce the gloom, arms raised before her face. She half walked, half ran, twisting away from low branches that scratched her legs and snagged her clothes. Firs and cedars, deeper black than the night, loomed up, receded. She heard an animal plunge away from her, its crashing movement sharp in the silence. She tripped, caught herself, was showered with heavy drops of moisture shaken from branches as she passed. Breathless, she stopped, bracing herself against a tree trunk until, in the darkness, the earth steadied beneath her feet. "This time," her grandmother had said. Supaya hoped fervently that she was right. If only she had her grandmother's heart! If only she would be found worthy!

Above her a bird called; another answered faintly, and she knew she must hurry to reach the hilltop before dawn. As the trees thinned out, she moved faster and was soon climbing the slope, slipping on the damp, loose stones that rattled under her steps. She felt for footholds and climbed over and around boulders, pulling herself steadily upward. Gasping for breath, she paused and, tilting back her head, saw the rocky summit silhouetted against the paling night sky and knew she had come too far. Skidding and sliding, she scrambled to her left and down and found the small pocket hidden between the boulders. She sank down on the patch of earth, dizziness momentarily overcoming her. Her pulse throbbed; her forehead was clammy. She had eaten nothing since midday the day before, and felt an empty, nauseating fear. Perhaps she should go back! Perhaps, like her older sister, Neegonas, she shouldn't try at all! Who knew what might happen! A terrible grinning manito might come to shake her senseless or fling her down the hill and break her hopes like poor Waboose, who hopped around the reserve on puny legs and never lifted her eyes. Yet Jacques, her brother, had fasted many times, had dreamed and been greatly blessed. And her grandmother, who cared for her, had wrapped her in the strength of her own shawl and given tobacco for her to offer. Regaining courage, she looked up and saw the stars glittering in their last brilliance before dawn and low in the west, the glowing sickle of the moon, hazy and faintly orange. She stood up and leaned against the huge rock, her hands resting on its cold surface. A faint wind cooled her forehead. Gazing upward, she felt her spirit drawn up into the boundless magnitude of the sky, into that majestic, eternal serenity stretching above the earth whose vastness diminished her world, made herself less than a speck. She became bodiless, drunk with space, enraptured with the immensity of the heavens, pierced by its awful beauty. Swiftly she took tobacco from a small pouch and, stretching out her arms, made an offering to the east where already night had faded, to the south, to the west where now only one horn of the moon shone above the distant edge of the lake, and to the north. Head flung back, she turned round and round to the four points of heaven as the paling stars swung above her and repeated the prayer her grandmother had taught her.

"Oh Great Spirit, hear me! The moon and stars
are yours! The sun that brings us life is
yours! The winds that blow are your breath!
All the earth, even the smallest stone, you
have made!

"All birds, beasts, people are yours! See me here!
I am yours! Without you, I am nothing.
Great One, help me! Accept my offering!
Show me the path that I must follow! Teach
me where to set my foot!

"Mighty Father of all, I bow before you, weak
and empty! Help me! Breathe upon me!
Make me strong! Make me worthy!"

Supaya closed her eyes. Unaware of herself, she
slumped down on the earth. She was floating, moving
effortlessly over a green meadow where sunlight sparkled in a meandering stream. There were women, talking and laughing together, picking berries and sweet
grass. All were dressed for a festival, their clothes em-
broidered with quills in the most glowing colors and
intricate patterns Supaya had ever seen. She moved
among them and put out her hand to them, but they
didn't see her. She thought one of the women was her
mother, but when Supaya spoke to her, the woman
smiled and moved on with her friend. Then clouds
covered the sun and all the women faded with the
sunlight. The meadow became a dark forest filled with
weird hootings and harsh cries. Frightened, Supaya
began to run, but the earth swerved up, the path vanished in thick undergrowth, and branches pressed suf-
focatingly about her. Her feet were too heavy to lift
and she cowered down against the earth. Abruptly the
branches above her parted. A huge bear loomed over
her, his massive body ringed with light, his eyes glowing like coals of fire. He swung his head and showed
his sharp, powerful teeth. His raised paws dripped red.
Supaya opened her mouth but could not scream. She

tried to raise her arms to shield herself, but a terrible numbness overcame her. The bear grew larger and larger until her weak sight could no longer encompass him, and she lost all consciousness. Then slowly her spirit revived and she awakened. Like a returning wave, her strength washed over her. A profound serenity filled her being. She saw that the bear was beckoning to her, and she followed effortlessly where he led, his radiant form illuminating the way. They emerged from the forest into a meadow where wild grasses rippled in a pale sunlight. The bear stopped by a tangle of bushes heavy with berries. Supaya saw then that his paws dripped with berry juice and understood that she was to eat the berries. They were juicy and deliciously sweet to her parched throat. As she ate, the bear's radiance grew brighter, more intense, blinding her eyes. Confusion overcame her. She covered her eyes, tried to turn from the light. Abruptly, she came fully awake.

The sky above the hollow was a thin, pale blue, its color washed out by the briliant sunlight that glanced off the boulders and shone on her where she lay on the ground. Dazed, she sat up, a memory of sweetness in her mouth. Suddenly she remembered. She had dreamed! She had been blessed with a vision! Exultant, she breathed in the fresh morning air and gazed at the world around her. Never, she thought, had a morning been so beautiful. Below her the stcep hillside still lay in shadow, its tumbled rocks like the humped backs of sleeping beasts. Beyond, the deep green of the woods extended unbroken to the waters of Georgian Bay, each pointed treetop distinct in the clear early light. And beyond the trees stretched the boundless water like a great bowl of gleaming silver, its far edge lost in a misty blue that melted, imperceptibly, into the blue of the sky. High above her a lone hawk floated, riding invisible currents, while over the lake gulls' wings flashed white as they circled about, weaving an endless pattern.

Spurred by her elation, Supaya made a wild, reckless descent, leaping and sliding over the rocks. She raced through the woods, now dimly lit by shafts of sunlight slanting through the trees. Touched by light, the ground fog slowly rose, curled, and faded away.

Supaya came out of the woods near the end of the garden. Smoke was rising from the stack in the lean-to roof. The back door opened and Jacques stepped out, carrying a pail. At nineteen, he was taller than his father but lanky, without his father's breadth. He stood for a moment, yawning and running his hand through his tousled black hair, then started toward the pump. Supaya ran toward him across the garden, leaping the rows of cabbages, potatoes and beans. Eyes shining, she exclaimed, "Jacques! I had a vision! I must tell Grandma and Father!"

She dashed through the door into the lean-to. Her father, his broad, muscular shoulders hunched, was leaning over the washbasin, splashing his face and hair. He held out his hand for the towel lying on the bench. Supaya snatched it up and handed it to him, biting her lip to hold in her excitement, impatient for him to look at her, to speak to her.

Jules toweled his face and head vigorously and took his time in speaking. His actions were always considered, deliberate, according to his nature and his profession as a shaman. Yet this deliberateness, Supaya knew, was deceptive. Powerfully built as he was, with massive shoulders and arms that in appearance matched his manner, he was more agile than most young men and could move with startling swiftness when he chose. This latent power gave him an air of mystery, of unpredictability that enhanced the respect with which he was regarded by all members of his band. And by his family as well. Though he often joked with her and Jacques and told them stories in the long winter evenings, some part of him remained aloof, closed off like a secret room where, since the death of his wife, no one had been admitted or would dare enter. For as long as she could remember, Supaya had been conscious of this reserve in her father. It had taught her respect and caution.

Jules, a handsome, square-faced man with pronounced cheekbones, took great care with his appearance. Carefully he combed his thick black hair, smoothing it back with a strong, well-shaped hand. He looked at Supaya through the mirror, amusement in his dark eyes.

"Good morning, Daughter. You were up early today."

"Yes, Father, I was."

Jules' amusement deepened. He turned to Jacques, just entering with the pail of water. "Jacques, your sister was up early this morning. Perhaps she was eager to hoe the potatoes."

Jacques' long, bony face broke into a wide grin. "Or pull weeds. That's the job she likes best."

Supaya tilted her chin at them pertly and turned away. She filled a large enameled pot with water from the pail and set it on the cast-iron stove.

"I can see she has nothing of importance to say," went on her father.

Quayo, hearing Jules' remark, exclaimed, "Shame! Can't you see the child will burst if you don't let her speak. Come, Supaya, tell us."

Eagerly Supaya turned, ready to share her experience with the three people she most loved. They all looked at her, smiling, waiting for her to speak: her brother, comically protective of her, but a young man with thoughts and hopes of his own; her father, whose humor she understood but whose depth of sadness eluded her; and her grandmother, the flame of life still bright in her eyes, upright despite the years on her back. Facing them, Supaya suddenly perceived each one in his own, individual, private separateness. All at once she understood why one who had dreamed

never blurted out the dream, understood the impro-
priety of such a blunt and personal revelation; and so,
almost embarrassed by what she had intended to say,
said simply," "I went to the hill before the sun rose.
My offering was accepted. I dreamed. I dreamed of
the Great Bear."

There was an impressed silence. They gazed at her,
marveling, and she felt their pride and happiness.

Her father said softly, "Ah! That is good. Very
good."

Her grandmother came forward and kissed her on
the forehead.

"At first," said Supaya, her constraint lessening, "I
was frightened, but then I wasn't."

Jacques patted her awkwardly on the shoulder with
his big hand. "I knew you would be brave. Now let's
eat. I'm hungry."

"You are always hungry," declared Quayo. "We
will have nothing left to store in the root cellar the
way you eat!"

Jacques caught Quayo round the waist and swung
her about. "Well, we have to celebrate Suppy's dream,
don't we?"

Supaya poured four mugs of green tea, got out some
leftover scone, and set it all out on the wooden table.
Besides Jules' straight chair with arms and Quayo's
rocker, both sitting near the fireplace, there were four
armless chairs, all of wooden frames with double-
woven splint seats, all chairs that Jules had made.
There were shelves on the wall holding tins of flour,
sugar, and tea, and pegs in the wall for holding clothes.
A bed for Quayo stood against the far wall, opposite
the fireplace, near a steep flight of steps leading to
the loft where Supaya slept and where food was stored.
Curtained off from the main room was the bedroom
Jules shared with his son.

Going into this room, Jules opened his trunk and
returned carrying a necklace of small gray stones with

a large, flat, translucent blue stone at the center. On either side of the blue stone was a single curved bear claw. Solemnly, with both hands, Jules held it up before Supaya. "This was given to me by my father. It has great power. Now I give it to you."

Awestruck, Supaya bowed her head and her father placed the necklace around her neck. When she looked up at him, her "Thank you, Father," faded away, for she saw that while he passed his hand lovingly over her head and gazed deeply into her eyes, he was seeing through her or beyond her, something or someone else.

As they drank their tea, there was little conversation. Her father and brother spoke of where they would fish that morning; her grandmother cupped her steaming mug in both hands and leaned her gray head over it as if to warm her sharp nose. Supaya, after her fast, was hungrier than Jacques and consumed her tea and dry scone with relish. She looked down proudly at the necklace, touching the cool, smooth surface of the blue stone. It gleamed softly and struck off an inner point of light like a tiny star. She was surprised by her father's gift. When Jacques had dreamed, Jules had given him a fine hunting knife of proved power, but as a girl, she had expected nothing.

After her father and Jacques left to go fishing, Quayo said, "Come, Suppy, sit down in front of me and I will comb your hair. It's snarled."

Supaya brought the comb from the wash bench in the lean-to and sat down on the floor, leaning back against her grandmother's knees. She liked the feel of the comb pulling through her long hair and the touch of her grandmother's hands smoothing and stroking it back.

"Grandma, tell me again about my mother. What was she like?"

"Ah," said Quayo, smiling. Quayo was the last of her family. Small but wiry and strong, she had out-

lived brothers, sisters, husband, and five children.
Fiercely proud, she had taken only one husband, finding no suitor who could rival the one she lost. Her
face, though lined by many sorrows, was animated by
an eagerness for life, and she delighted to speak of her
lost daughter, to make her live again for Supaya. "Your
mother was a dutiful, loving daughter. She was always content and was kind to the old people. They
would say, 'Here comes Shooskonee, bringing us food
again.' She had a gift for life. Her garden was always
the finest, her bread the best. Her hands were clever.
Her quill embroidery was something to be proud of.
Your father, who could have had any girl on the reserve, chose her, and she was a good mother to your
sister Neegonas and to Jacques. She was very sad to
leave you, newly come into the world."

Supaya listened with pleasure, but she was remembering her dream. "Did she wear her hair straight back,
without a part, in a knot on her neck?"

"She did. She had long, glossy . . ."

"And did she have a dress with a square neck and
quill embroidery on the shoulders?"

Quayo didn't answer immediately. Supaya felt her
grandmother's sudden attention in her silence and the
arrested movement of her hands, and heard the question in her voice when she answered, "She did."

Supaya twisted around to look up at Quayo. "I saw
her, Grandma." Quayo took Supaya's face in both her
hands and looked at her searchingly. "I am sure I
did. She was laughing and happy."

"She thinks of you and loves you, Suppy," said
Quayo. "Some day you will see her again." Then,
briskly, "Now turn around and hold still while I make
a part."

Supaya turned and held still, feeling the tooth of the
comb draw a line across the middle of her head and
the pull of her grandmother's fingers as she swiftly
braided one side. Supaya ventured one more question,

tinged with mischief, knowing the reaction it would provoke. "Grandma, is it truly a good thing to have dreamed of the Great Bear?"

"Supaya!" Her grandmother gathered the other half of her hair in one hand and pulled her head sharply round. Her old eyes narrowed sternly and she solemnly held up one hand. "Ah! Ah! Do not question! You have been very blessed. You have been given one of the most powerful spirits for your guardian. Never forget your dream! Remember it always! If ever you need help, you can ask Him, your Grandfather."

"Come, now. Enough talk. Let me finish. I have preserving to do and you must hoe the garden."

Supaya followed her grandmother into the kitchen. Quayo put more wood in the stove and got out a large kettle. For the first time Supaya saw how small and frail her grandmother was. The house itself had grown smaller since she had left it, only hours earlier. Everything was altered, for she had dreamed, had seen beyond these walls. Now she saw with older eyes.

She fetched the hoe from the barn and began chopping at the weeds, breaking up the hardened earth around the half-grown vegetables as she had seen Quayo do. There was much work to be done before her father and Jacques returned with their catch.

CHAPTER TWO

Buttoning her jacket against the chilly, mid-September breeze, Supaya hurried along the dirt road toward the schoolhouse. Skipping a step or two, she could feel the blue stone of her necklace bounce against her chest. She had worn it ever since her father had placed it around her neck and had promised herself never to take it off. It was her dearest possession, an object of awe and veneration carrying as it did the love of her father and grandfather and a great mystical power through which she could draw closer to her guardian spirit. It warmed her soul as the sun was even now warming her back.

The day was fine for drying squash and beans. She was late because she had stayed to help cut and spread them out, knowing her grandmother would fret if the work were not done. Finally, "Go now," Quayo had insisted. "I will finish. You must learn what you can for your own use."

Kineu, she knew, would have waited for her at the crossroads. He never cared if he was late for school. Sometimes Supaya thought Kineu didn't care whether he learned to read and figure the white way or not, even though he learned faster than she did. But she cared. She had watched Mr. Bonnet, in shirtsleeves and suspenders, leaning on the counter of the general store, adding up their purchases. He jabbed his pencil at each figure in the column, then looked unsmilingly at her over the rims of his eyeglasses and announced

the total in a voice that made Supaya wonder if what
her grandmother claimed were true: that he charged
them more than the figures really came to. She determined that one day she would be able to tell. Besides,
there were magazines and books with pictures that
stirred her curiosity, pictures of white girls in strange
white hats with ribbons, walking on beaches, holding
hoops or strings attached to balls floating above them.
When she asked Miss Harris what they were doing,
the answer always was, "Now when you can read,
you won't have to ask such questions."

Rounding the bend, Supaya saw Kineu at a distance, tossing his knife at a fence post, and she quickened her step. For her, everything quickened in Kineu's presence. The very day itself expanded, for his
liveliness and enthusiasm made their wildest projects
seem possible. For him all difficulties melted away. Today they were to go fishing. Supaya was eager to sell
some fish to make money in order to buy her grandmother a new shawl.

Catching sight of her, Kineu came to meet her.
Tall and slim, he walked with the springy step of a
runner. His features, still boyish, were finely cut, his
nose straight, his mouth modeled with a natural sweetness. Supaya always thought of him as moving in sunlight.

"I have the boat, Suppy," said Kineu, falling in with
her step. "We can take it all day if we want."

"Then we can go right after school. No, first I must
go home and tell Grandma. Then we can go."

"We can go now."

"*Now*," said Supaya, "we must go to school."

Kineu was silent. Head down, he concentrated on
kicking a stone ahead of him. Supaya glanced at him
sideways, knowing he was disappointed, that he would
rather do anything than go to school, that school didn't
matter to him as it did to her. It upset her when they
disagreed. Her Aunt Hettie, Kineu's mother, often

shook her head over them. "Those two! Like an old man and an old woman, they think alike. What next!" But about school they did not think alike. Finally she said insistently, "We must learn."

Kineu stopped and faced her, his eyebrows straight and serious. "Why? Books don't catch fish."

Supaya frowned, at a loss to explain Mr. Bonnet's figures, the mysterious lure of books, the elusive world of little girls in big hats. Baffled but stubborn, she said, "I must," and hung her head.

Kineu, unable to cause her pain, began walking again. "All right. We go after school. We can meet at North Point. I have a net set out there." He pretended not to see her happy, grateful smile.

The schoolhouse, built according to government regulations by the Ojibwa themselves, was a one-story rectangular building with the door at one end, rooms for the teacher to live in at the other, and windows along both sides of the single large classroom. It was a plain, solid building, an extension in board and brick of the character of their teacher, Miss Agatha Harris, unimaginative but practical and dedicated to good hard work. Steps—convenient for the posing of class photographs—led to the door where Miss Harris would stand and ring a hand bell as part of her effort to instill in her students a respect for time, marking off the moment before which they were "on time" and after which they were "late." To all such efforts they remained impervious. Those who were not smitten by strange, sudden illnesses or detained by work that "had" to be done, came when they comfortably could, arriving by two's and three's during the course of the morning. Between turning to the blackboard, chalk in hand, and turning back, Agatha would find her class had changed, increased, rearranged itself. Yet from the oldest to the youngest, their faces showed such uniform bland innocence that it was impossible for her to scold them. She believed it was deliberate, this refusal to conform to time, a stubbornness of character, and she included in her morning prayers a special plea for help in dealing with this perverse, pagan trait.

Sophia Cedar and Kenneth Bruley appeared as if by magic in the middle of a lesson. The younger children, in a group at the front, were copying the alphabet while she put addition problems on the blackboard for the older ones. She turned and there they were, in their seats at the back, as calmly attentive as if they had been there for hours.

Agatha's normally pale cheeks flushed with irritation. She had not even heard the door open and shut; a small detail, but it made her feel all these children slipped through her hands as they pleased, no matter how she strove to organize them. She was utterly baffled by what she conceived to be the Indians' total lack of discipline. For four years now since, at twenty-one, she had come to Stone Island, Agatha had determinedly struggled to change it, yet could see no improvement. She refrained from speaking to Sophia and Kenneth's families because these two late-comers were her best students. Kenneth was bright; he simply treated school work as an unimportant game which he wasn't much interested in playing. Sophia Cedar was bright also, and in her Agatha sensed a drive to learn that set her apart from the others and made her progress a source of particular satisfaction. If only the girl's grandmother were stricter with her.

Agatha, telling herself she must be patient, tried to ignore her irritation and a growing headache. She had skinned her straight, light brown hair back too tightly. Her scalp felt taut. For one absurd moment she yearned to undo it and shake it down around her shoulders, to loosen the high collar that seemed to constrict her throat. Abruptly she became aware of rows of solemn, fathomless dark eyes, all fixed on her, and she came stiffly to attention, tapping the board with her chalk.

"Sophia Cedar, come to the front and do these problems. The rest of you do them in your notebooks. Then we'll go over them together."

Reluctantly, Supaya went to the blackboard. She wished Miss Harris had called on Kineu instead. He never minded being watched while he worked.

The class bent their heads and began, sneaking looks now and then at Supaya's answers. Miss Harris walked between the rows, observing her students' work. A slim young woman in a tight bodice and long skirt, she bent over their notebooks with them, smiling encouragingly, tapping a finger at doubtful answers, raising her eyebrows at others.

Supaya was almost finished when the door opened and Reverend Harris walked in. It was his pleasure to visit the schoolroom occasionally, believing it to be rightly part of his domain. He often found his young sister too soft in her attitude toward these children, and frequently had to strengthen her discipline. At sight of his stout, aggressive figure, the class immediately grew wary and bent their heads lower, elbows angled out defensively on their desks.

"Class, say good morning to Reverend Harris." The class responded in a monotone, and Agatha smiled to turn it into a welcome. Though it pained her to admit it, her brother's presence sometimes made her uncomfortable. But this morning his appearance steadied her. His absolute self-assurance simplified her problems, drew a sharp, clear line between right and wrong.

Not for years had Reverend Harris smiled spontaneously or looked with gentle affection at any living creature. The onerous demands of his calling did not allow for it. His sense of heavy responsibility permitted no more than a benign skepticism. He strolled between the desks, nodded at the tops of bent heads, his hands stroking his lapels as if smoothing down dull, black feathers. "Doing sums, I see. Good. Good. And your letters. Commendable, very commendable." He had into the habit of repetition under the impression saying a word twice made it more understandable. He approached the front of the room, his pale eye busy noting uncombed hair, a dirty shirt, empty seats. His glance flicked over the blackboard. "I see Miss Cedar is leading the . . ." He broke off, stared for one horrified moment at Supaya, then raised an arm as if to ward off what he saw. His stunned silence and dramatic stance caught everyone's attention. All heads raised. Even the two youngest, Anna and Marie, who had been slyly poking each other, stopped to watch.

"Nathan," asked Agatha, startled into using his given name in public, "what is it? What's wrong?"

Reverend Harris' face twitched with the anger that swelled within him. His voice was hollow with outrage. "How dare she wear those pagan stones? How dare she! Why have you allowed it? What kind of example is she setting for these children?"

Momentarily confused, Agatha pressed her hand against her throat. Then she saw Supaya's necklace, the gleaming blue stone and the sharp bear claws, startling against the faded print dress. "Oh but . . . she only just . . . I mean, she had her back . . ."

"There is no excuse! No excuse!" the preacher exclaimed furiously, staring at Supaya, who had backed up against the blackboard.

"No! No, of course not!" agreed his sister miserably.

"Responsibility such as ours demands constant vigilance! Constant! Now, Miss, what do you mean by adorning yourself in such a manner? Well? Speak when you are spoken to!"

Speechless at being the focus of such anger, Supaya stared back, wide-eyed, too frightened to look away.

"Ha!" He pointed a finger at her. "She understands well enough! The devil has easy work here! But we will defeat him! Take off that heathen charm! Remove it! Give it to me!" He held out his hand imperiously.

Aghast at his demand, Supaya clasped the blue stone against her chest and backed away. She was conscious of Miss Harris gesturing nervously, of the tense stillness of the class, of the bars of sunlight falling across the desk tops, of Kineu, who had risen, silently opened the door and was waiting, his hand on the doorknob.

"You dare defy me!" Reverend Harris' voice rose in pitch. "You are a child of the devil! You defy the word of the Lord!" He was suddenly beside himself with rage at this child, at her grandmother and her father, all stubbornly practicing their pagan religion and doctoring behind his back, all refusing to bend to his will, all undermining the authority of the church. "Give it to me!" he demanded, biting off his word. "Right now!" And his outstretched hand made a swift grab for her.

But not swift enough. Sensing his action, Supaya dodged past him, ran down the aisle and through the door, past Kineu, who slammed it shut behind them. Together they fled down the steps and ran without pausing until they were far from the schoolhouse.

"Come on!" Kineu was standing on a rock, his back to the lake. They had come through the woods to the shore, and he had been pitching stones, waiting for her to recover. Supaya sat on the beach, hugging her knees and sulking. I will never go back, she thought. How I hate him! That she wanted to go to school made it worse. But she would not take off her necklace, not even for school.

"Come on, Suppy!" Kineu called again.

She raised her head and saw him balanced on a rock, smiling at her, his hair shiny black in the sun, behind him the light blue sky, the deeper blue lake. Poised thus, arms out, he seemed to her enviably free and light, as though he could fly away. She looked at him wistfully, but didn't move.

Suddenly he slipped and fell, arms thrashing. "Ow, ow! My leg! Ow!"

Instantly Supaya was on her feet, running to him.

"Kineu! Are you hurt? Oh, let me see!" But as she leaned over him, he stopped yelling and grinned up at her.

"Oh, Kineu!" She stood up and looked at him sideways, but in a moment she laughed too, unable to resist his smile.

"Come on! We can go fishing now! We'll have time to sell some!"

They raced along the shore to where the rowboat was drawn up on the shingle. Above the waterline, near the trees, was a small storage shack. There they left their shoes and together pushed the boat into the water.

The lake was icy cold and so clear that along the shore the sun shone into it, lighting up the stones on the bottom that seemed to ripple under the water. White gulls with black-tipped wings dipped in the sky above them, outriders of a flock that was circling another, larger fishing boat farther out on the lake.

"I row first, then you, while I haul in the net." Kineu braced his feet and pulled strongly on the oars. The wind was biting fresh over the water and Supaya sat with her feet up on the seat to warm and dry in the sun.

"Better than school?" asked Kineu, teasing.

Supaya made a face at him. "Only if your net has been lucky and caught many fish."

Near the mouth of an inlet Supaya took over the oars. The water here was choppy and the boat bucked sideways in the current.

"Start on this side," said Kineu, and Supaya rowed to one end of the net floats that were bobbing up and down in a crooked line across the inlet mouth. Leaning over the side, Kineu began hauling the linen net up and into the boat. Caught by their gills in the net, fish came up shimmering through the water, suckers, white fish, and lake trout. Some hung dead, but most flopped and arced their bodies violently as they came over the side, showering water in all directions.

"Hey, hey!" cried Kineu, disengaging a trout, "that's a big one! And another!" Every pull on the net brought up more. Kineu worked skillfully and rapidly, using a stick to kill the live fish by a blow on the head. Water dripped from his arms, soaked his shirt and pants, and sloshed in the bottom of the boat. When the net was all in Kineu sank down on the seat, breathless, and surveyed the pile of fish, their sides iridescent in the sunshine.

"We got a good haul, Suppy!" he exclaimed jubilantly. "We never caught so many at one time before! We should get good money for these. Two, three times more like this and I will have plenty for my gun."

"And I can get Grandma a shawl!" Ever since the day of Supaya's vision when Quayo had given her her own shawl, Supaya had wanted to get her a new one. She had already seen just the one she wanted on a shelf in Mr. Bonnet's store.

"Your necklace brought us luck, Suppy," said Kineu.

In the excitement of hauling in the net, Supaya had forgotten Reverend Harris and her own fright and anger. Now she pulled vigorously on the oars, heading for a small island out in the lake, half a mile beyond Stone Island. She no longer worried, confident that when she told her father what had happened, he would know what to do.

They reached the island and tied up at a small jetty built out from the rocky beach. The water sparkled and lapped gently against the poles driven into the lake bottom. Children playing along the shore called out excitedly and came running. Two women appeared, coming from houses set well back in a clearing. The children crowded along the jetty, curious to see what Kineu and Supaya had brought. Kineu lifted up two large fish, a whitefish and a trout, for the women to see, then laid them down on the wooden planking.

The women admired the fish, and the older woman, who was stout and talkative, sent one of the children racing back to her house. She smiled down at Supaya. "You are Jules Cedar's girl, I know. He has given you his eyes. He is a fine doctor, a good man. He cured my son when he was a baby and very sick. He is strong now, but a no-good. Wants to play all the time." She laughed and tousled the hair of a boy standing beside her. "Here," she said, counting out some coins from a little bag the child had brought from the house. "When you have more fish, come back. We have a big hunger here."

As Kineu untied the boat and pushed off, she called out, "Old Aunt Theresa lives round the point. She would be happy for some fish."

The point extended into the lake like a crooked arm, forming a small, sheltered bay. Stunted, wind-bent pines grew far out on it, fighting for a hold among the boulders. Behind them were slender larches and cedar groves, forming a windbreak for the small frame house that sat back from the beach. At one side was a partially cleared area where a garden barely survived among the weeds. Beyond were a few old apple trees, their branches heavy with apples.

Kineu ran the boat up onto the beach, its bottom grating on the stones. Smoke rose from behind the house and from the smokestack, but no one appeared.

"We should go to the door. She may be asleep."

The front door stood ajar, and from the step they could see into the room, empty except for a bed, a small wooden table, and two straight chairs. Across the room, another door opened into the lean-to. They heard the creak of a rocking chair. Supaya knocked on the doorframe. There was no answer and the rocking continued. "She must be hard of hearing," said Supaya, entering and calling loudly, "Aunt Theresa! Aunt Theresa!"

Supaya need not have feared startling Aunt Theresa. When they entered the lean-to, her eyes were on them. She was an old, old woman, beyond surprises. She seemed to have been expecting them, and her face, despite its deep wrinkles and sunken cheeks, expressed an almost youthful anticipation. "*Ahnee*," she said, nodding, "*ahnee*. Come in, children come in. I have some bread out in the fire. If you bring it in, we can eat. My old legs are tired."

In the backyard a fire smoldered under an old broken drying frame. Kneeling, Supaya raked through the ashes and charred wood with a branched stick and pulled out two loaves crusted with ashes and bits of wood. She whipped the loaves with a switch and then, using a stick so as not to burn her fingers, knocked off the cracked crust. She rolled the hot loaves into a fold of her skirt and carried them inside.

"Open that box there," said Aunt Theresa, as pleased as a child at a party. "We will have meat and tea." Kineu cut the bread and got dried meat from the tin. Supaya poured tea from an old pot heated on the iron box stove.

"Aunt Theresa," said Kineu, "we have fish. Would you like some?"

Aunt Theresa looked at him keenly, then pointed at the bread. "Eat," she urged, "eat."

"I think she is deaf," said Supaya. "You hang some fish to dry and I'll pick apples."

Kineu nodded, and Aunt Theresa, drinking her tea and rocking, smiled at them slyly like an old conspirator.

When they finished eating, Kineu repaired the drying frame, setting in firmly the slender branches that slanted up on two sides to the center pole that was held parallel to the ground, and retying the basswood fiber ties that held the cross branches in place like the skeleton of a tent. He gutted the fish on the beach, sloshed them in the water, and cut a slit along each side of their spines so they could be hung lengthwise over the poles, first flesh side out, then skin side out, until they were dried. As Kineu slit and hung the fish over the cross poles of the frame, Supaya took an old splint basket and went out to the apple trees that stood knee-deep in weeds. A squirrel, who had been carrying off apples one by one, sprang away, flicking his tail and scolding.

Aunt Theresa came to the door and watched them work, nodding her head and mumbling to herself. When Supaya brought back the basket filled with apples, Aunt Theresa picked out a large one, rubbed it against her skirt and presented it to Supaya. "Good little woman," she said, chose another, rubbed it, and handed it to Kineu. "Good little man."

Eating their apples, Supaya and Kineu walked along the curving shore out toward the point, where the beach narrowed and finally disappeared altogether, the land falling steeply into the lake.

"Look," exclaimed Supaya, pointing, "you can see the hill above the trees!" To the east, Stone Island, bathed in the late afternoon sun seemed to hover in the crystal air. Supaya, squinting against the sunlight reflecting off the water, gazed at it, rapt, as if she were again standing on its summit.

Kineu understood. Beginning at the age of seven, he had gone out in search of a vision, and one morning when he was ten, on the far side of the same hill, after a three-day fast, he had dreamed. He would never forget the splendor of that morning, that place, or the elation he had experienced. Since then he had walked with pride, at home in his world. He knew Supaya's guardian was the Great Bear, as his was the Eagle. He crouched down at the water's edge, idly flipping stones, liking the feel of their cold, grainy surfaces. One caught his attention.

"Suppy! Look! Look what I found!" He held out on his palm a curiously shaped stone, rounded and lump-ish, like the body of a sitting bear.

Supaya leaned over it, awed. It was sitting, slumped a bit to one side, and there was its head, its snout and tiny rounded ears. "Kineu!" she breathed, "a bear!" Their eyes met, hers filled with wonder. Suddenly all the events of the day became significant: they had led her to this, this sign. She was almost frightened, as if the Great Bear had reached out and touched her.

"Here," said Kineu softly. "It is yours to keep."

Slowly Supaya reached out for it. It was cold and heavy and had dried to a pale gray with rings of darker gray circling it. She held it on her palm, then closed her fingers over it and put it in the pocket of her skirt.

That evening Supaya told her father what had happened at school. Jacques sat cross-legged by the hearth, breaking small branches and sticking them into the flames that crackled and gave welcome warmth on a fall evening. Her grandmother and father had drawn their chairs close. The rest of the room was in shadows. Above them, Joe Crow, her father's pet, paced back and forth on a ceiling beam, cocking his eye at them and making soft croaking noises. As Quayo listened to Supaya, her mouth drew tight. She had opposed Reverend Harris since Supaya's sister, Neegonas, had abandoned the old ways. She rarely attended Sunday service, excusing her absence by saying she was too old. Supaya was always amused to see how feeble her grandmother became whenever the preacher called.

Jules listened impassively, his eyes fixed on the flames. When she finished speaking, there was a deep silence until Joe Crow suddenly swooped down onto Jules' shoulder and pecked delicately at his shirt button. When Jules turned his gaze on Supaya, she saw the anger in his eyes.

"You did well to leave. I would not have you go back to that school."

"Pah!" exclaimed Quayo, unable to keep silent longer. "That white woman knows nothing! What is she good for? Nothing!"

"It is also good for him that the preacher did not strike you or take your necklace," continued Jules, ignoring Quayo's interruption. "He does not understand that we know nothing of his devil, just as he knows nothing of the One who watches over us. But you will come with me to service on Sunday so he will know that we are not afraid of his devil or of him."

"Father," said Jacques, "if she does not go to school, the agent will send her away to a government school, especially since Mother . . ." His voice trailed away at a sharp glance from his father. "Oh no!" exclaimed Supaya, alarmed. She leaned toward her father beseechingly. "Father, please don't let them send me away! Please!" Knowing his dislike of tears, she blinked hard and kept her eyes steadily on his.

Jules regarded Supaya thoughtfully. He saw her fear and her effort at self-control. "But the necklace—you will then take it off?"

His question startled Supaya. She stared at him, then sank back on her heels. Stubbornly, she said quietly, "No, Father, I will not."

"Ah," said Jules, deep satisfaction in his voice. After a moment's silence, he spoke again, straight-faced. "Then I see what you must do. You must wear your necklace under your blouse. That will be one more thing the preacher will not know."

His sudden change of tone surprised them all. Jacques looked up and laughed; Quayo threw up her hands, smiling and nodding. Joe Crow, reacting to their mirth, stretched his head forward and cawed.

As they all watched, Supaya solemnly lifted the blue stone and the bear claws and slipped them under the neck of her blouse. Then they all laughed together.

That Sunday Reverend Harris faced his Indian congregation and preached to them on the sinfulness of pagan adornment. Stones, feathers, claws, teeth, all were an abomination unto the Lord and were not to be endured. He spoke of the wicked, rebellious hearts beating beneath their Sunday shirts and dresses, of the sinfulness of the old men holding their good black hats on their knees and the old women in their shawls who per-

sisted in their heathen customs. He threatened them
with eternal hell's fire if they did not bend themselves
to the yoke of the Lord and do His bidding.

His audience listened placidly, attentive and non-
committal, sitting on benches they themselves had made,
in the spare, unadorned church they had built. But
when Mrs. Harris, plump and tightly corseted, struck
the opening bars of the closing hymn and led the singing, they joined in enthusiastically, enjoying a good sing.
If the sermon was directed specifically at the Cedar family, sitting upright in a back row, no one in the congregation appeared to be aware of it.

A week later on the steps of the general store, Agatha
Harris almost collided with Jules Cedar. She had been
hurrying with her head down and stopped just short of
running into him.

"Oh, pardon me, Mr. Cedar. I wasn't looking where
I was going." He stood on the step above her, his face
shaded by the wide brim of his black felt hat. He nodded politely and stepped to one side as if to go on his
way.

"Mr. Cedar." He turned, and she felt the impact of
his full attention. Immediately she was thrown into confusion. "Mr. Cedar, I've wanted to speak to you for
some time . . . well, that is . . . since last week . . ." She
stopped, overcome with embarrassment. He waited silently for her to continue, his dark eyes on hers. Their
penetration, their knowingness scattered her wits. She
felt he understood precisely her agitation.

"I mean . . . your daughter, Sophia, has been absent
a whole week." She hesitated. He offered no comment.
"I hope she hasn't been ill." He still said nothing, but
his eyes, seeing every aspect of her face and person,
grew softer and darker, and she began to babble. "Well
. . . she . . . she must come. That is . . . it's the law . . .
as I'm sure you know . . . not that I . . ." She stopped
again, her burning cheeks betraying her response to

his masculinity. If only someone, anyone, would come by, would interrupt them! But no one did. In her need to cover her embarrassment, Agatha blurted out, "I hope she'll come back next week!"

At that Jules' eyes widened slightly and the faint smile at the corner of his mouth deepened. He tilted his head toward her and said with quiet emphasis, "Thank you, Miss Harris. Supaya will come." Touching his hat brim, Jules walked away.

Agatha looked after him, her cheeks still warm. If, sometimes, during the years that followed, there was a suggestive contour under the neck of Supaya's dress, Agatha Harris was careful not to notice.

CHAPTER THREE

Above the treetops all across Stone Island Reserve thin columns of smoke rose into the still, clear air of an autumn morning. Behind every home, fires burned under drying frames hung with split fish and strips of meat. Hides were stretched out for scraping and tanning. Garden vegetables were stored away in log-lined root cellars or were drying in the sun before being wrapped in birchbark to be stored for winter use.

In the garden, now gone to seed, Jules and Jacques were digging the last of the potatoes. Supaya worked along behind the men, gathering the potatoes into a basket and carrying them to the root cellar. All morning her body had felt tired, listless. Stooping made her head swim and her stomach cramp. She straightened up, and after another brief twist of pain, felt a wetness between her legs. Abandoning the basket, she stepped quickly across the dug-up garden and entered the house, giving Quayo, who was sitting outside the back door, a sidelong glance as she passed.

Quayo was stringing apple sections to be hung for drying, but she noticed Supaya's strange look and how she avoided passing near the apples. Putting aside her work, she went in and found Supaya waiting for her near the front door.

"Grandmother, what you told me would happen, that soon I would become a woman, has begun. I must go into the woods."

Hearing the tremor in her voice, Quayo touched her gently on the arm and reassured her. "Do not fear. It is natural that girls grow into women. You wait here. I'll get Neegonas. We'll make you a shelter."

Supaya's sister Neegonas and her husband lived in their own log house a short distance down the road. Neegonas had one child, a boy of three, and was pregnant again. A short woman, inclined to stoutness, she was of a generally jolly disposition now that she had her own home in which to do as she pleased.

When Quayo returned with Neegonas, Supaya fell in behind them and they crossed the field at a distance from Jules and Jacques and headed toward the woods. Supaya turned her head so as not to contaminate her father and brother by even a glance and followed the two women into the woods until they were well beyond sight or sound of the house.

"I think it was about here that I came," said Neegonas, and remembering, giggled and patted her swelling belly. "We'll have to find you a husband soon, Suppy. Or maybe now he will find you."

Supaya said nothing. She was uneasy and vexed by her sister's teasing. She had never been close to Neegonas and wished she and her grandmother could have built her shelter by themselves.

"Do not tease her, Neegonas. She is not like you. Here, this is a good place. Go and cut some branches." A large downed fir lay at an angle across a rockfall. Branches slanted across one side of the trunk and over the rocks would form a kind of cave with the rock at the back. "Suppy, you cut some cedar."

Neegonas swung her axe resentfully. She had never pleased her grandmother, who had always ordered her about, made her chase after Jacques and tend the baby, Supaya, after their mother died. No one thought of her. She had been made motherless too. She brought the branches and placed them at a slant, thrusting their cut ends into the earth. "I suppose you think Kineu won't come after her now? And all the others?" she asked, intending to hurt.

Quayo was on her knees, spreading cedar boughs on the ground inside the shelter. She looked up at Neegonas sternly. "Think what you say. She is your sister."

Supaya stood apart, her back to them, shoulders drooping, head bent. Neegonas felt a touch of shame. "I will bring a blanket and some food," she said, and went back the way they had come.

"Supaya," said Quayo, "come. Sit inside."

Supaya stooped under the branches and sat down on the cedar boughs, her back against the rock.

"See, you have room to lie down."

"Yes, Grandma." Supaya said nothing more for fear she would cry.

When Neegonas returned she brought an old blanket which they spread as a covering over the branches. She handed Supaya a box with some dried meat and scone in it. "You will be hungry later."

Supaya held it on her lap, self-conscious and awkward. "Thank you, Neegonas," she murmured, not raising her eyes.

Neegonas straightened up. Her back ached and she was impatient to return home.

"I'll bring you another blanket and water before dark," said Quayo. "Now we must go."

For a long time Supaya sat without moving, the box still on her lap. The impulse to cry had passed; now she felt only a strange emptiness. She looked down at herself. She could see nothing different, yet her body was changing, whether she wished it or not, mysteriously, by itself. She had been so happy, so content, in the pleasant, unchanging "now." Life might change for others, but hers had been secure and uncomplicated. Now she too was being swept along as

Neegonas had been, as her mother, as, so long ago, her grandmother . . . reluctant and unready.

She put the tin box down and moved as far back under the branches as she could, wanting to hide herself. She took the stone bear from her leather pouch, cupped it in both hands, and addressed it silently. Oh, Grandfather! Help me! Make me strong enough to become a woman!

She spent all day leaning against the rock, watching the angle of light change where it fell on the ground before the opening. Ants toiled up and down a crevice in the rock. A squirrel carrying a nut in his mouth ducked under the branches, cocked a startled eye at her, and raced out. When the light began to fade, Quayo returned.

"Come," said Quayo, urging her out. "Stand up and put on your jacket. Drink this tea and eat. Then you will feel better. Here is a blanket to wrap up in."

The tea warmed Supaya and made her realize how hungry she was. She ate some of Neegonas' dried meat and bread. "Grandma, could you bring me some work to do tomorrow? It is hard to sit doing nothing all day."

"Yes, Suppy, I . . ." Quayo broke off and listened. They heard voices and laughter. Then three young men came into view, carrying fishing lines and strings of perch and sunfish. The first one noticed the women, stopped, and said something to the other two, who turned their heads.

Supaya stared at the ground. Quayo stepped in front of her and regarded them sternly; she knew them all since they were children. As they hesitated, she raised her arm and pointed in the direction of their homes. They exchanged glances and sly grins, then moved quickly out of sight.

"Now," said Quayo, "we will make up a fire." Together they cleared a space and laid a fire. Soon the pungent odor of burning wood and leaves hung in the damp, dusky air. The cracking, leaping fire was reassuring, and Supaya knelt down close to it, knowing that her grandmother would return home, the fire would burn low, and she would be alone.

Quayo, looking at her across the flames, saw the fear in her eyes and understood. Supaya had heard women telling tales, Neegonas among them, of their times in the woods, how young men, daring each other, had broken the law and taken them against their will. Quayo got to her feet. Light was almost gone, and her old eyes no longer saw well in the dark. "I will go now. Do not be afraid. Stay in your shelter. Jacques will guard you."

Supaya watched her grandmother go, then crawled under the branches and curled up in her blanket, lying so she could see the glow of the fire. In one hand she held the stone bear close to her cheek. Once during the night, she roused The fire had died. A heavy ground fog filled the woods. The only sound was the quiet drip of moisture from the trees.

Morning light came slowly in the woods. Supaya, waking early as usual, lay snug in her blanket until the fog, struck by sunlight, slowly began to lift and fade away. She was sitting cross-legged eating bread when her grandmother came.

Quayo was out of breath. "*Ahnee,* Granddaughter! You see, I pant for your sake! You give my old legs exercise."

Supaya laughed and hugged her grandmother. One night was safely past. With the coming of daylight, her fears seemed foolish, esepcially now that Quayo was come and they sat together drinking hot tea sweetened, as a treat, with maple syrup. Supaya's spirits rose and she asked eagerly, "What did you bring for me to do?"

From her basket Quayo took out a bundle of old clothes, scissors, needle, and thread. "Here, cut these up and sew them together. You'll soon need a new cover for your bed."

Left again by herself, Supaya began cutting up the clothes. Some she recognized as her old dresses, handed down from Neegonas or her grandmother, or as her father's or Jacques' old shirts. Others were strange, and she knew they had been sent to the reserve by white people. She worked contentedly, making neat stacks according to color and pattern, cutting away the worn parts. She worked steadily all morning and afternoon, the sun warming her back and lighting up the brilliant red and yellow leaves that lay in drifts against the dull brown leaves of past years. Now and then she heard the chatter of a squirrel, the hard drumming of a woodpecker, the strident call of jays, or a rustling in the underbrush that was suddenly stilled, surprised by her presence. Once a small, brown-patterned snake, scarcely discernible amid the leaves slid into view, pulled back its head to consider her briefly, then glided away. She stopped to eat and to drink some water and, thinking she heard whispering voices, climbed onto the rockfall and stood for a time above her shelter, looking in all directions. But she saw no one, and coming down, began sewing the patches together.

That evening, after the deep orange sun had disappeared behind the darkening trees, her grandmother returned, bringing food and water. Together they made up the fire and Quayo rested beside it before going home. She was pleased with Supaya's work.

"Ah, Granddaughter, you will have it half pieced when you come home."

Now that night had come again, Supaya was once more filled with dread, remembering the voices she was sure she'd heard. The time when she could go home seemed very far off. "I wish . . ." she began, then stopped, ashamed of her lack of courage. She saw Quayo's old eyes, bright in the firelight, watching her, waiting for her to continue. Supaya smiled and shook her head. "Nothing, Grandma."

But Quayo understood. She stroked Supaya's hair and said to encourage her, "Your father misses you. He has already gathered the rocks for your steam bath."

When her grandmother had gone, Supaya put more wood on the fire, crawled under the shelter, wrapped herself in the blanket, and fell asleep.

She was startled awake by the sounds of drunken voices and bodies crashing through the underbrush. Alarmed, she moved as far back from the opening as she could, pressing herself against the rock. In the dark, she could see nothing except the glowing embers of the fire, but she could hear movement, exclamations, low laughter.

"There! That's her fire. I told you."

"You sure no one's guarding?" A second voice.

"Ah! You're crazy! Give me the bottle!"

"Shut up!" A third voice.

"But her father's a doctor! And that old woman might be a witch!"

"I told you, shut up!"

There was a scuffle, grunts, a thud, then ominous quiet. Supaya scarcely breathed. Tense, she listened for the faintest sound, stared wide-eyed into the dark to catch the slightest movement. Where was Jacques? Had he heard? Was he near? Suddenly a shadow passed between her and the fire. A tipsy voice spoke.

"Come on out, Supaya! Let's be friends. Come on, let's have a little fun!"

"Come on, we know you're there. We'll see if you're a woman yet!" Laughter, and another shadow crossed in front of the fire, blocking out its glow.

"Hell, we'll make you a woman!"

"Maybe you want us to drag you out!"

Then Supaya remembered the scissors. Stealthily she felt for them in the dark. Touching the cold metal, her fingers closed around the handles and she held the scissors raised, poised to strike like a knife.

"Yeh! Drag her out! What're we waiting for!"

Branches were shoved aside from above her. A solid, breathing body lunged forward. Hands grabbed for her. With a strength born of fear and defiance, Supaya slashed out with the scissors. Instantly there was an agonized yell. The hands fell away as the man reared violently back and crashed off into the brush.

At the same moment there was another yell and the crack of a fist against bone. Supaya was on her feet, ready to run, as another body, arms flailing, sprawled backward onto the fire.

"Yiiiiii!" Screaming, he rolled over, thrashing his arms and legs. Supaya, horrified, saw Jacques, his face briefly illuminated by the firelight, fall on him and beat him furiously. Suddenly out of the dark a third man flung himself toward Jacques' back. Supaya saw the glint of a knife and screamed a warning as another man leaped forward and grabbed the arm holding the knife. Under his impact, they all crashed down together, kicking and twisting. The burned man squirmed from under, and getting to his feet, rushed off. The others struggled, hands reaching for the wildly jabbing knife. It arced downward, there was a sharp cry, then a yelp of pain as Jacques caught the knifer's arm and twisted it viciously. The knife fell, the last man grabbed it up, and for a moment all three were still, panting for breath, Jacques holding his attacker against him from behind.

Keeping his hold, Jacques spun him around and thrusting his face close, said softly but distinctly, "Next time . . . I kill you." Contemptuously he thrust him away. The man stumbled backward, caught his balance, and paused, calculating his chances. But he was uneasily aware that the other, unknown man who had his knife was somewhere in the dark, waiting. With a snarl of disgust, he turned and ran.

The fire was scattered. The woods were unusually still as if even the trees were listening, waiting. Jacques, his face grim, swept the embers together and added wood. As the fire took hold, he saw beyond the flames Supaya's hand at her side, still clutching the scissors, its points dark and wet. Without looking up at her, he said quietly, "You are a brave . . . woman. Are you all right?"

In a few deadly minutes Supaya had become a stranger to herself, but she managed, through numb lips, to answer, "Yes." Then added, in a whisper, "Thank you, Jacques."

Jacques stood up, careful to turn his back to Supaya, and said, "Kineu, I owe you my life."

Then the other man stepped forward out of the dark. Unlike Jacques, he looked directly at Supaya, and she saw with a shock that it was Kineu. But he was not the gay, laughing Kineu she knew, not the boy she had grown up with, gone fishing and hunting with, shared secrets with. Seen across the flickering firelight, he was as much a stranger to her as she now was to herself. His eyes were narrow and angry, his mouth tight and hard. Blood ran down from his slashed cheek. He stood silent, staring at her, his hand still murderously clenching the knife.

"Kineu," said Jacques, striving to divert his gaze, "Kineu, they won't come back now." He laid his hand on Kineu's arm. "Come, let's repair the shelter." He moved to pick up the branches. "Lie down, Suppy."

Supaya closed her eyes for a moment, shutting out Kineu's bleeding face. Then, dazed, she lay down against the rock and wrapped herself in the blanket, pulling it forward to hood her face. The scissors she kept beside her. Gradually she relaxed. She could hear Jacques and Kineu moving about, rebuilding the shelter. With the rock at her back and the branches above, Supaya felt once more enclosed, protected. She fell asleep listening to the murmur of their voices.

Two days later Quayo fetched her home. They went together to the barn, where Supaya undressed and wrapped a blanket around herself, then to a small lodge made of curved saplings covered with blankets.

"It is all ready," said Quayo. "Your father heated the stones and I brought water from the spring. The steam will make you clean."

Supaya lifted the flap and stooped inside. She handed the blanket back to Quayo and lowered the flap. Naked except for her blue stone necklace, she knelt down on the cedar boughs which had been spread beside the white hot stones piled to one side. They had been sprinkled with water from a basin and steam filled the small interior. It filled her lungs and made her eyes sting. But the penetrating, moist heat warmed her to the bone and relaxed her muscles. Breaking off some tops from the cedar boughs, she flicked more water onto the stones, then stretched out her arms and rubbed them with the aromatic leaves. Their scratchiness made her damp skin tingle and come alive as if, like the snake, she was shedding her old skin for new. She arched her back and rubbed it, then her neck and chest and saw, almost with surprise, that her breasts were round and full. Turning sideways on her hip, she extended one leg and languidly rubbed the cedar over the curve of hip and thigh. For the first time she recognized the beauty and grace of her body and apprehended all at once its possibilities. She looked upon it in wonder, as on a strange, new possession, all the more remarkable in that others might desire it. Suddenly she felt a stir of pride, a new energy. Kneeling back on her heels, she looked down at the symmetry of her body and touching the blue stone that lay cradled between her pointed breasts, she whispered, "Thank you, Grandfather, for helping me become a woman."

That evening the family sat by the fireplace, eating popped corn and drinking tea. Quayo, in her rocker,

sat closest to the fire, a shawl about her shoulders.
Jules puffed on his pipe and stroked Joe Crow's glistening black feathers. The bird perched firmly on
Jules' knee but his bright eye was fixed on Jacques,
who now and again tossed him a grain of corn which
he caught expertly and swallowed with a satisfied gulp.

Supaya, handing round the corn and keeping the
tea cups filled, was conscious of her changed position
in the family and of their eyes upon her, full of love
and quiet pride. She felt a shy but giddy happiness
and smiled irrepressibly at the slightest remark. And
they, fondly amused, laughed with her as if they all
shared a delightful secret.

"Today," remarked Jules in an offhand manner, "I
heard from the wind in the trees that it is no longer
safe to go into the woods." He paused, face solemn,
eyebrows slightly raised. "I hear there is a terrible
beast there who spits fire and strikes with claws of
steel. It must be so, for I saw at the store one man
whose back was burned and another whose arm had
been slit from elbow to wrist. One must be very careful of angering such a fierce beast, eh, Joe?"

Joe Crow cocked his head wisely and chuckled,
"Awk, awk, awk," and they all laughed. Later, from
her bed in the loft, Supaya gazed out at the moon-
less, windy night. All were asleep, and the house was
quiet. The fire had burned out and Joe Crow, full of
corn, had gone to roost on a beam. Secure once more
in her home, Supaya was content, but her happiness
was tempered by the sober realization that no more
could she rely utterly on father, grandmother, and
brother to care for her, or follow their directions with
no thought of her own. Now she must assume respon-
sibilities, behave like the young woman she had become. Thinking of her grandmother, strong in spirit
but frail in body, and of her widowed father whose
loneliness she only now was beginning to appreciate,
Supaya was filled with gratitude and a great resolve.

She would work harder. She would show them how much they had taught her, and try to care for them as they had cared for her. She would make them proud of her.

And then she thought of Kineu. She had asked Jacques about him, and he had told her Kineu was well, that his face was healing. Tomorrow she would see for herself. She had known Jacques would protect her; he was her brother and nearly twenty, but Kineu . . . She remembered his face as he had looked at her that night across the fire, and smiled to herself in the dark. She was changed; he must also have changed. No longer did she feel empty. The Great Spirit, wise in all things, had blessed her with a great contentment. She lay back and fell asleep almost at once, eager for the morning.

CHAPTER FOUR

During the night a heavy fog rolled in from Lake Huron, blanketing all the west side of Stone Island, an isolating, silencing fog that chilled the bones of the old people. Supaya made up the fire in the stove, and her grandmother stood by it holding out her arthritic hands. She fretted about her cousin, Emilia.

"Auntie Em will be hungry. There is no one to make up her fire."

"I will go, Grandma. Here, drink your tea."

"But the fog is bad."

"It won't last," said Jules. "The sun will eat it up and give us a fine day for hunting." He and Jacques were leaving to check their traps and go hunting. The garden had done well that year. The root cellar was well stocked with vegetables and the loft with dried fruit. But although many fish and much meat—raccoon, rabbit, and deer—had been dried, there was not enough meat to carry them through the long winter.

"Maybe I'll bring you a good fat porcupine, Grandma," said Jacques.

"Then I will make you a fine stew, Grandson. May you be blessed in the hunt."

By the time Supaya started for Auntie Em's, the sun had risen above the trees, its glowing face as pale as the moon's. But the fog had begun to lift, moving slowly in ghostly, tattered clouds. Supaya, holding a pot of soup in one arm, walked along the road where the fence posts and trees, dripping moisture, appeared, then disappeared, and the stone church, the preacher's house, and the schoolhouse seemed to waver and shift about. Passing the schoolhouse, its row of windows pale yellow squares, Supaya felt a twinge of regret and was glad that Miss Harris, should she glance out a window, would not see her going by. Supaya was now fifteen and had not returned to school. She had completed the fifth reader and had done so well that Miss Harris had asked her to help teach the beginners their letters. But though she wanted to learn everything Miss Harris could teach her, she wanted even more to learn all that Quayo knew. Already Supaya did most of the cooking and preserving and all of the sewing. And Quayo had taught her how to make birchbark boxes and do quill embroidery, for which she now had such skill that she'd been able to sell them to Mr. Bonnet. She could add now as well as he, and one by one she had read all the books Miss Harris had on the shelf in her bedroom. Most of all, she wanted to learn how to heal. Quayo was teaching her what she knew of herbal medicine, and she was learning more from other old women who gave her recipes in exchange for food or a quill box of unusual design. Auntie Em knew little medicine, but she was older than Quayo and lived alone. Supaya often took her food, made up her fire, cleaned her house.

Auntie Em lived beyond Mr. Bonnet's store, and as Supaya approached the store and dock area, she saw that the trim little lake steamer had arrived and was docked alongside the government wharf, the lines of its steel-plated prow and smokestack softened by the shifting fog, heavier over the water. She heard raised voices and the thuds of crates and barrels being trundled down the gangplank and over the hollow-sounding boards of the wharf. The double doors of the general store were propped wide open. Mist swirled and gleamed in the pale light slanting out across the porch.

Mr. Bonnet, in a long apron, his shirt sleeves tucked up, waved his arms and shouted directions. White men with faces permanently reddened from raw weather and wearing knitted caps, heavy jackets, and boots went back and forth between wharf and store, rolling barrels, carrying boxes or burlap bags slung over their shoulders. Several Indian men lounged on the porch rail that dripped moisture, their black hats set low on their heads, watching, perhaps waiting for the mail-bags to be opened. Few passengers arrived this late in the year, but two Indian women, carrying carpetbags, and a small child stood to one side, waiting patiently for a friend or relative.

Supaya, hurrying past and thinking to avoid the path of a man carrying a barrel on his back, dodged behind him and ran directly into another man who appeared unexpectedly out of the mist. She cried out as her hold on the pot slipped. They both grabbed for it, their heads almost colliding, and caught it to-gether.

"Well, well!" The man laughed and straightened up, the pot held between them. "A double catch! My lucky day!"

Supaya had seen a few white men—Mr. Jackson, the Indian agent, Mr. Bonnet, the sailors—but never one like this. Unaware that she was staring, she stared. His black suit was stylishly fitted. The brim of his hat curved smartly over curly hair and brows nearly as black as her own. His fancy vest was a brocade and adorned by a gold watch chain. As he smiled down at her, Supaya was struck by the solid, physical force of him, but most of all she was startled by his vividly blue eyes, by their intense directness.

Jess Fallon was used to coquettish glances, but open amazement was new to him. He was surprised by the beauty of this girl, the high, smooth brow, wide cheek-bones, and large, slanted dark eyes. The unconscious wonder in her expression, in her soft, slightly parted lips, touched him, stirring in him a sudden wish to detain her, to come to know her.

Realizing she was staring, Supaya started to back away and only then saw that his hands covered hers as together they held the pot. Overwhelmed with embarrassment, she lowered her head and gave a tug on the pot.

Instantly he removed his hands. "Excuse me, ma'am," he said, and she heard the laughter in his voice. "Could I carry it for you?"

Without raising her eyes, Supaya shook her head and walked rapidly away.

Auntie Em's little one-room frame house was surrounded by trees on three sides but faced with the rocky shoreline and caught the full force of whatever weather swept in off the lake. She was awake when Supaya knocked but still in bed, trying to keep warm under an old quilt. The fire in the small iron box stove was out, and the room was cold.

"*Ahnee,* Auntie Em." Auntie Em made an effort to sit up. "No, no. Stay there until I have made up the fire. Grandma sent you some soup."

"Ah, you are so good to me, so good!" She lay back and watched as Supaya made up the fire, brought in a supply of wood and a pail of fresh water from the pump.

"Now, Auntie Em, would you like to sit in your rocking chair? I'll comb your hair. Then you can have some hot soup. Here, let me help you up." Because she had broken her hip the previous winter, Auntie Em limped and moved with difficulty. She leaned on Supaya and settled gingerly into her chair near the stove. When she had washed and had her hair combed, Supaya ladled out the soup.

"Please, sit down. Sit!" Auntie Em insisted as she

began to eat. She smiled slyly at Supaya. Several of her teeth were missing, and the gaps gave her wrinkled brown face a mischievous, impish expression. "You are a fine young woman. When will you marry, eh? Do not shake your head. I hear things," Auntie Em assured her, nodding, "I hear!" She ate carefully, her bony old hand trembling as it raised the spoon.

At her words, Supaya thought instantly of Kineu, the image closest to her heart, the secret motivation for all she did. Since becoming a woman, she was not allowed to be alone with him, and he had stopped school the year before she did. But they saw each other often in the company of their families. Kineu often came home from hunting or fishing with Jacques. Kineu was no longer a boy, his father, Arthur, said, but a man, since he could now wield an axe like a man. Kineu's powers as a hunter and fisherman were well known throughout the reserve, it being rumored that his blessings gave him a knowledge of the likeliest places to set his nets and place his traps. His guardian was said to guide his aim, so accurate was he with knife and gun. He was most at home, Supaya knew, when hunting or fishing, most happy and alive when free to lie back on the earth and watch the clouds move, or to climb a hill and gaze across the treetops, or to pit his skill against that of an animal or the treacherousness of winter. He would be gone sometimes for days on a hunt, but always when he returned, he brought something for Supaya, often a porcupine so she might have the quills. At the fall fair he won all the races, being blessed with swiftness, though he laughed and seemed to care no more about winning than he had about learning to read. Nothing delighted Supaya more than hearing him praised, but she tried to hide her pride in him as she did her pleasure whenever he teased her, dropping her eyes whenever she caught him staring at her.

"Ah! You smile," said Auntie Em suddenly. "You

think of him," she added knowingly and with satisfaction.

"Auntie Em, your bowl is empty. Do you want more soup?"

"I know what young women think," she insisted. "I remember well."

"Auntie Em, do you want more soup?"

"No, no more. All the same, I know . . ."

"Here, Auntie Em, let me tuck your shawl around you."

"You are kind to an old woman," said Auntie Em. "I will not forget what you do for me."

Supaya bent and kissed her soft cheek. "Jacques will come later and cut more wood for your fire."

On her way home, Supaya saw that the steamer had loaded mail and passengers for its return trip and gone. The sun had burned away the fog, making the air warmer and luminous. Mist still glimmered far out on the lake. Crates were stacked on the ground in front of the store. Mr. Bonnet's son, a thin young man with the washed-out hair and pallid skin of his father, was carrying them inside one at a time. Mr. Bonnet himself stood on the porch talking to the man in the black suit, who stood with elbows out, fingers hooked in his vest pockets, nodding affably as Mr. Bonnet spoke.

At the sight of him, Supaya felt a mixture of embarrassment and irritation. She should not have run into him or been rude and tongue-tied when he offered to help her. But also he had caused her to stare at him like a foolish, brazen girl and, worse, he had been amused. She saw his head turn in her direction as he caught sight of her. Determined to maintain her dignity, she passed coolly by, skirting the crates and looking straight ahead as though no one there were worth her notice.

But he turned so as to keep her in view, admiring her carriage, the sheen of her long, braided hair, the proud angle of her chin. He listened to Mr. Bonnet, but his eyes followed Supaya until she was out of sight.

In late afternoon, when the sun hung low and blood red in a pale, cloudless sky, Jacques burst into the kitchen where Quayo was mixing bread and Supaya was sewing beads on a new pair of moccasins.

"Grandma, Suppy! Come! Father shot a bear!"

Both women dropped their work and rushed out after him. Jacques had gotten a porcupine and three beavers in his traps, but they were almost forgotten in the excitement over the bear, rarely found on their island. It was a large black bear, its pelt thick for winter and its body rich in fat. Before skinning it, Jules cut off its paws, feet, and head. The head he stuck on a stick driven into the ground near the fire. Supaya ran to the house and fetched red yarn which she wound decoratively about its head and ears. Quayo brought a pouch of choice tobacco which Jules sprinkled on the fire before the bear. As the fire crackled and the smoke curled up and around the bear's snout, Jules offered up their thanks.

"Great Bear, you have blessed us. You have guided us in the hunt. You have given us yourself that we may live.

"Great Bear, we, your brothers, thank you. May our offering give you pleasure."

Then he and Jacques skinned the body, putting aside the heart and liver which Quayo carried into the kitchen and put in a pot to be cooked. Daylight was fading fast, so they hung the porcupine and the beavers by their hind feet from a tree, leaving their skinning for the next day.

They were eating fish and fried scone when there was a knock at the front door. Cyrus Red Sky and his wife Miriam stood on the doorstep.

"We have come for the doctor," said Cyrus.

"Come in," invited Jules, "come in and sit down. Jacques, bring chairs. Quayo, some tea."

Jacques brought the chairs near the fireplace, then knelt by the hearth and made up the fire. Miriam sat down as though her legs would no longer hold her and gripped the ends of her shawl in tight fists. Cyrus, a large, heavy man, moved with dignified restraint to a chair, sat down, and carefully placed the large bundle he carried on the floor beside him. Neither spoke, but there was pain in their eyes; their silence was tense with worry that all could feel. Not until the tea had been served did they speak.

"My son Angus, my firstborn, is sick. You are a good doctor. We want you to make him well again."

"What is wrong with him?" asked Jules.

"His throat is tight. He cannot swallow. His body hurts. His skin is hot."

"Oh!" exclaimed Miriam, leaning forward and clasping her hands. "He is on fire!" Having broken her silence, she was unable to restrain her tears. Her husband turned and looked at her, whereupon she sat back and drew her shawl about her head.

"I will come," said Jules. "Tomorrow evening."

"I am glad. We will have a sweat lodge ready for you. These things I have brought now." Cyrus picked up the bundle and, unwrapping it, took out a plug of tobacco which he presented to Jules and then a new blanket. Having given his gifts, he stood up. "We will go now."

Next morning light was slow in coming. A gray sky had drawn down close over the land and the lake, turning the water to cold metal. Jules, preoccupied with preparations for the curing ceremony, withdrew into himself. He spoke to no one. He tasted no food.

Taking a special birchbark container sealed with resin, he walked far into the woods to a spring that bubbled up at the base of a slope. On such a still, gray day he could hear the murmur of its voice before he came upon the small, marshy pool it formed from a source that never completely froze over. Here Jules knelt on the wet, grassy margin and leaned forward, head bowed, arms extended out over the clear water that rippled up from the center and spread in widening circles. Swaying, he chanted softly. From the edge of the pool he scraped up mud and drew two smears across his forehead. Taking some of his own tobacco from his pouch and some that Cyrus had given him, he sprinkled both on the water and prayed.

"Oh Great Manitou, who gives us water that we may live, hear me! Accept my offering! Grant my spirit strength to drive out evil!

"Great Manitou, let your water soothe one who is sick! Accept this, his offering! Refresh his soul!

"Oh Great Wolf, my Grandfather, give your power also to this medicine, that it may carry your strength through his body! Renew his life!"

Holding the bark pail to the lip of the spring, Jules filled it, then rose and returned home. When he came out of the woods, Quayo was gathering up the bones of the bear and those of the beavers—Jacques had skinned them and stripped their flesh—and she was putting them into a bag to be hung from a tree that they might again be of use to the bear and the beavers. Supaya was pulling the quills from the porcupine. Jules passed them all without a word or glance and entered the house.

Using his own special bowls, he made a mixture of dried herbs from his own collection, slippery elm bark and checkerberry leaves, moistened it with the spring water and made a paste. This he covered and put to one side along with the container of water, a small wooden drum covered with stretched hide, and his otter skin medicine bag. Then he undressed except for a loincloth, wrapped himself in a blanket, and sat down cross-legged on the floor of his room, pulling the blanket down over his face.

Pulling quills was careful, tedious work. Pulling each quill out by its tip, Supaya sorted them according to their length, placing to one side those over three inches long and thus too coarse for fine embroidery. Quayo helped Supaya finish while Jacques turned over the strips of meat drying on the frame and kept the fire smoking. As Supaya was tying the quills into bundles, Kineu appeared, his gun in one hand, a large fat porcupine in the other.

"*Ahnee*, Aunt."

"Welcome, Nephew."

"I see you've been lucky," said Jacques.

"Yes. This porcupine put himself in my path, begged me to shoot him."

"Why, Nephew, why?" asked Quayo.

"Well," said Kineu with a serious face, but looking sideways at Supaya, "news has spread of wonderful embroidery being done here, of an artist of such skill that any porcupine would be honored to be put to such use."

Jacques and Quayo laughed.

"Here?" Supaya looked around. "I know no one of such skill here."

"Ah, I was mistaken then." Kineu turned to go.

"Wait, Nephew, wait. I will take him since no one else wants him," said Quayo.

"Such a poor porcupine. I cannot think who would want him," said Supaya. "He must be sick."

"All the same," said Quayo, holding the porcupine

over the fire, "I will just singe his nose and eyes so his soul will be at rest."

Kineu, standing near Supaya, noticed the backs of her fingers, scratched and bleeding from pulling quills. He took the singed porcupine from Quayo and, sitting down beside Supaya, pulled the quills himself.

Quayo spoke of the cure to be held that evening at the Red Skys'. As she talked, Supaya stole long glances at Kineu. His thick, black hair sprang back from his forehead and lay in shaggy ends against his neck. His lashes were long as a girl's, and his mouth, in repose, had such sweetness that she yearned to touch his face. At that moment, he raised his head and looked at her. Caught out, she blushed and dropped her eyes, hearing with pleasure Quayo assuring him that they would see him that evening at the curing ceremony.

By evening the wind had risen and was moving the slate-bellied clouds swiftly across the leaden sky. It churned up the lake, dashed the waves into spray against the rocks, and bent the pines, singing through their branches a song of coming winter. Jules strode ahead by himself, wrapped in his blanket, his medicine bag hanging from his belt. Quayo, Supaya, and Jacques followed, the women bending their shawled heads against the sharp wind. Jacques, carrying the birch container of spring water and the drum, walked with dignity as the doctor's helper, proudly, head up, his long hair flying in the wind.

Behind the Red Skys' house a sweat lodge had been erected, covered with pieces of canvas and a blanket. Near it blazed a fire, its flames wind-whipped. As Jules approached, Cyrus, using the crossed ends of two tied sticks, lifted fist-sized rocks from the flames and carried them, one at a time, into the lodge, putting them in a pile to one side of the cedar branches covering the ground. Jules, indifferent to sharp air, spread out his arms, putting back his blanket, which Cyrus re-

ceived and held for him. Jules stooped and entered the
lodge, lowering the flap behind him. With a cedar
whisk, he flicked water from a pail onto the hot, hiss-
ing stones until steam filled the lodge, enveloping,
warming, and purifying his body.

Jacques and the women went inside the house. Only
the fire in the fireplace illuminated the room. Its
beamed ceiling and corners were lost in shadows. Relatives and friends had already gathered, sitting on the
floor in rows along the sides and ends of the room.
Some stood, their backs against the walls. Unmoving
and silent, like dark-robed statues they waited, filling
the room with a portentous expectancy. The firelight
gleamed in their steady, meditative eyes, threw into
light and shadow their grave, strong-boned faces. Only
when a newcomer entered did they move, nodding
their heads in silent greeting.

As in the center of a stage, the patient, a boy of
sixteen, lay on a woven mat of cedar bark in the
middle of the floor. His face, turned from the fire, was
in shadow. But all could see the labored rise and fall
of his chest and hear the shudder of his breathing. His
mother sat near him, head bowed, hands tightly
clasped. High on the stairs leading to the loft her two
younger children sat close together, their eyes wide and
solemn. Jacques waited near the door for Jules. Quayo
and Supaya joined those along the side. More people
arrived, among them Hettie, Jules' sister, her husband
Arthur, and Kineu. Kineu quickly picked out Supaya.
Edging his way through, he reached her side, and they
sat down together on the floor, their backs against the
bottom stairstep.

After that no one else came. As the waiting was
prolonged, the tension increased. No one spoke. No
one moved. Only the patient stirred, turning his head
restlessly.

Suddenly a draft of cold air swept into the room.

Jules entered. Instantly all eyes turned to him, held by the dynamic, compelling power of his presence. He stood with his fierce intense gaze fixed on the patient, oblivious of the rows of people in the shadowed room.

Moving swiftly, he jerked back his head, threw off his blanket, and taking up the drum, gave it one slap, an ominous, opening note. A deep thrill ran through the watchers. Raptly they followed every move. Leaning forward, knees bent, Jules moved slowly toward the patient, lifting his feet in time to the rhythm he tapped out on the drum. He began to chant, his voice at first so faint and deep that the listeners couldn't tell when it began but felt it like a song that had risen from deep inside themselves. Four times he circled the patient, his gaze concentrated on him. Gradually the tempo of his drumming increased to a continuous, insistent beat, and his chanting grew louder. As he circled about, firelight glistened on his bare back, arms, and chest and flashed on his beaded apron. Suddenly he fell to his knees by the patient and with one swift gesture threw back the quilt. He drew from his medicine bag a handful of earth, and gently rolling the boy to one side, spread it under his back. Then with head tilted back and eyes closed, Jules resumed his chant, drumming with both hands on the drum held between his knees. His voice rose from deep in his chest, resounding, vibrating, filling the room with his supplication. The audience, entranced, swayed with the rhythm, following every modulation of his voice.

After one long, tremulous note, he abruptly stopped. He put aside the drum and laid his hand on Angus' forehead. He took from his bag a box of mixed herbs and stirred them into a bowl of the spring water. He dipped his fingers in it and bathed Angus' head and throat, stroking firmly up and down. The boy responded with a kind of groaning sigh. Lifting Angus' head, Jules held the bowl to his lips. At first the water trickled down the side of his chin, but Jules persisted. Finally, the boy's lips moved, he made a faint effort to swallow, painfully, several times.

A low sigh rose from the audience; there was a stirring among them. Miriam raised her head, the beginning of hope in her eyes. Kineu inched closer to Supaya, pressing his shoulder and arm against hers. Her eyes fixed on her father, she pretended not to notice but was careful not to move away.

Jules set aside the spring water and opened a box containing the paste. He rubbed it on the boy's chest in rhythmical, circular movements, then on his arm and leg muscles, massaging and flexing them. Gently he rolled him over face down, stretched his arms beyond his head, and rubbed the paste into the muscles of his back. The aromatic smell of checkerberry filled the room. Rolling Angus onto his back again Jules once more gave him the herbal water to drink. This time Angus weakly opened his eyes.

"Drink," said Jules, and Angus drank. "Now sleep and be healed," said Jules, covering the boy with the quilt. Angus' eyes stayed open, gazing vaguely upward. Jules began to chant again, softly, accenting the rhythm with a beat on his drum. Slowly, Angus' eyes closed, his head tilted to one side, and he slept.

Jules rose and increased the tempo of his drumming, singing softly but confidently, stepping in time to his beat. He sang at Angus' left side, then at his feet, at his right side, and finally at his head. His audience moved with his rhythm, their dark faces flushed in the firelight, their eyes glowing. As he circled round and round, his enlarged shadow slid across the beams, shot up into dark corners, came tamely back to his measured step. Finally he stopped at Angus' head, sank to his knees, lowered his head, and extended his arms over the boy. A pulsing silence filled the room. Moisture glistened on Jules' broad, curved back. His powerfully muscled arms vibrated, merging the power of the watchers with his own, concentrating all the tension, focusing it, stretching it, holding it taut, suspended.

Suddenly, just before the breaking point, his muscles went slack. His body sagged. He stood up, arms hanging wearily. Jacques stepped forward, holding up the blanket. Jules wrapped himself in it, covering his head, and quietly left the house. Quayo, Supaya, and Jacques, carrying the drum and container of water, followed him. Only then did the guests rise and, nodding at Cyrus and Miriam, silently depart.

All the next day Jules stayed in his room, resting and fasting, drinking only water from the spring. At dusk, on his way back to his patient, he saw that the wind still blew from the west, a good portent for Angus' recovery.

Angus was awake when Jules and Jacques arrived. Unobtrusively, Jacques placed the drum and water near the pallet and went to sit with Cyrus and Miriam. Jules felt Angus' forehead and again bathed his head, neck, and chest with spring water and held his head while he drank the herbal water. Then from his medicine bag Jules took a small bundle of birchbark, unwrapped it, and took out a piece of dried *weekan* root.

"Chew this slowly until it is all gone."

Obediently, Angus began chewing as Jules drummed and danced, chanting a low but vigorous song, turning in tight circles as he described a larger circle about the patient. As he danced there was a knock on the door. Before Cyrus could reach it, the door opened and Reverend Harris stepped inside.

"I heard . . ." he began, and stopped, staring amazed at Jules, now still as stone, at Angus, looking up wide-eyed, at Cyrus and Miriam. Anger rose like a blush in his face. "What is going . . . how dare you carry on these pagan rites!" Furious, he turned to Cyrus. "I have forbidden this! Your son needs a doctor, not a quack!"

Sullenly Cyrus thrust his hands into his pants pockets and said nothing Miriam, frightened, lowered her eyes and clasped her hands nervously together. Jules glanced at Jacques, who picked up the drum and birch box and brought Jules his blanket. They moved quietly toward the door, but Reverend Harris, infuriated by such lack of response, burst out at Jules.

"You! You defy me! You defy God's word, time and again! You and your whole family!" He raised an angry fist. "You are undermining my work here, and for that you will feel God's wrath! You will burn in hell for this!" He made a move to seize the drum and birch pail from Jacques, exclaiming, "I'll burn these heathen . . ." But Jules swiftly thrust out his arm in front of Jacques, and leaned toward the preacher, his face threatening, his eyes narrowed. "It is you who should beware!"

Reverend Harris jerked back. "Don't you dare touch me!"

Jules' lips curled with contempt. "You understand nothing!" He spat out his words. "You are cold, empty! Leave this house! Go back to your god and pray for him to enlighten you!"

Stunned, his mouth dry, Reverend Harris looked to Cyrus, to Miriam, but they stared at the floor. Struggling for self-control, he could find no words, no way to oppose Jules' bitter scorn. Baffled, he turned and rushed out of the house.

Miriam raised her head, looked from her husband to Jules, neither of whom moved or spoke. Full of distress for her son, she beseeched Jules to continue. "Please! We beg you! Continue!"

"Not now," said Jules, turning away. "For now I am done. I will come again tomorrow."

The next evening, Angus was propped up on one elbow, drinking broth. Jules gave him more root to chew. Then he burned tobacco in the fireplace and sang a song of thanks to the Great Manitou and to

his guardian, the Great Wolf. When he finished, he
broke his fast, eating the dried meat and bread Miriam
brought him.

"You have made my son well," said Cyrus. "We
will have a celebration."

For the next several days Miriam and her sister-in-
law busied themselves preparing for the feast. They
made fruit pies, venison stew, and corn soup. Cyrus
killed a pig, scalded it, scraped off the bristles, and
cut it into large pieces for Miriam to roast in the
oven. They borrowed an extra table and extra chairs.
And on the day itself, the women heated quarts of
berries in maple syrup and baked bread and fried
scone.

The day was ideal for a feast: the air crisp and
cold, invigorating for playing ball, the sky a fragile,
cloudless blue with no hint of bad weather. The intense reds and yellows of maple and birch flamed
against the deep green of fir and cedar.

Walking along the road with Jacques behind their
father and grandmother, Supaya breathed deeply the
tingling, exhilarating air and felt so happy with her
world, so buoyant, that she wanted to spin in circles.

"What are you smiling at?" asked Jacques.

"Ah!" exclaimed Supaya, flinging out her arms. "At
the beautiful world! At you! At everybody!"

Jacques laughed. "I know. You like going to a
party because you like seeing Kineu."

"And you," teased Supaya, "like seeing Maud!"

"Oh ho! I'll get you for that!" cried Jacques, chasing
her.

Supaya sprinted ahead. caught her father's arm, and
danced along in front of him. "Save me!" she cried,
laughing, "save me!"

Jules smiled and put an arm about her shoulders.
"You are saved!"

Peering over her father's shoulder at Jacques, Supaya made a face.

"Be careful," warned Jacques. "You'll be caught when you don't expect it!"

At the crossroads they met several other families, and all walked on together. As they approached Cyrus' house, they could hear voices and smell the tantalizing aromas of roast pork and bread mingled with that of burning wood. Men stood around a large, outside fire, smoking their pipes and talking. They raised their hands in greeting to the newcomers. Children raced about, dodging their elders, dashing into the house and out again. A white spotted dog, his tongue lolling, chased after them, confused by their shifts in direction. By the door a group of young women had gathered. They watched Jules approach with sly, admiring glances.

He was greeted formally at the door as the guest of honor. "Welcome to our home," said Cyrus, ushering him inside. "Please sit here by the fire," said Miriam.

Quite aware of the young women's admiration, Jules entered with an easy dignity and accepted a chair. Relatives and friends stood back, leaving a small space around him for the payment of gifts. Cyrus and Miriam brought him another blanket, a large tin of tobacco, a sack of flour, and a quilt with a pieced design and red yarn ties. Angus, who was still resting on his cedar mat in the corner, came shyly forward. He carried a new pair of winter moccasins decorated with beadwork, and these he held out to Jules.

"Please accept these. I hope they will ease your path."

"I will wear them with pleasure," said Jules.

After the payment, formalities were forgotten. Guests crowded around the tables, helping themselves to the food, urged by Miriam to fill their bowls again and again. Women went back and forth, replenishing the food in the bowls and stirring the pots that steamed on the kitchen stove.

Supaya joined the group of young women standing outside. They were laughing and talking among themselves while watching the young men who had started a ballgame in the field across the road. The players raced toward one goal, swerved round toward the other, scattered and converged, intent on their pursuit of the ball. Old men leaned on the fence and watched, smoking and laying bets.

Maud stood with Supaya. She was a small, shy girl, several years older than Supaya. As a schoolgirl she had admired Jacques and had dropped her large eyes to hide her pleasure whenever he had singled her out. Recently he had made his preference for her quite clear and she felt herself trembling on the edge of a great happiness, waiting for the day when Jacques would ask Jules to speak to her father.

"Your brother plays very well," said Maud.

"Mmm, yes," answered Supaya, her eye on Kineu, who could outrun all the others.

"I prefer the father," said Rhea, boldly.

Startled, Supaya turned to see who was so presumptuous as to openly refer to her father. Rhea was a girl Supaya knew only by sight. She was nineteen and had left school earlier than most of the other girls. Supaya had seen her at the store, flirting with Mr. Bonnet's son. Now she ignored Supaya, gazing past her at the players. The bland innocence of her sloe eyes and smooth, oval face, the little knowing smile curving her large sensuous mouth indicated an experience superior to that of the others.

"I hear he's been visiting the Widow Walker," said Rhea pertly. Embarrassed by Supaya's presence, none of the girls spoke up. Supaya looked stonily away, hiding her shock by pretending not to have heard.

"Oh well," said Rhea with a shrug, "she's too old. I bet he'd like someone younger." Some of the girls giggled, and Rhea tossed her head impudently. "You can have the boys. I want a man," she said and went inside.

"Do not listen to her, Suppy," said Maud softly so the others wouldn't hear. "She has a big mouth and will say anything."

Supaya nodded, but for her the celebration was ruined. She was sickened and humiliated to hear her father so spoken of. She wanted to go home, to draw her family close around her. She wanted what Rhea had said to be untrue. She left the group and went around to the back of the house, hoping to find Quayo. Quayo was in the lean-to, conferring with several other women over a piece of sewing one had brought. Through the door Supaya could see her father. He was standing with his back to the fireplace, smoking and talking to Mr. Jackson, the Indian agent, a stout, middle-aged man whose wide stance was partly for effect and partly for balance. He was explaining something with gestures and Jules was listening, looking down, a faint, thoughtful smile on his lips. Supaya started toward him. Then, as the people crowded around the tables shifted, she saw that his glance rested on Rhea, who sat in front of him, daintily eating a piece of pie and listening to his conversation, her coy eyes, shadowed by her long, loose hair, fixed on his.

Instantly, Supaya turned away and, seeking comfort, went to stand near her grandmother, but Quayo was absorbed in her own conversation. Feeling strangely dislocated and lonely, Supaya wandered outside and stood for a while watching a group of children down on their knees in a circle, playing with three moccasins and a shell, vying with each other, guessing in which moccasin the shell was hidden.

As the sun sank behind the trees, the evening grew chill. People drew closer to the fire. The ballgame came to a shouting finish, and the players came trooping back, thirsty and hungry. The old men argued over the plays and exchanged tobacco to pay off their wagers.

Rhea, seeing that Jules' conversation was going to continue, had risen and with a lingering glance at Jules, had gone outside. Jules was discussing with Jackson woodcutting privileges on the reserve when Cyrus joined them. Jackson nodded affably at his host. A single man, he enjoyed celebrations. And like a single man with no restrictions beyond those in the government handbook, was blunt and often unconsciously tactless. Over the years his manner, like his girth, had steadily broadened.

"My brother Wenonga is coming for a visit," said Cyrus. "He sent a message through my sister-in-law. He will come on tomorrow's boat."

"Wenonga!" said Jackson thoughtfully, as though this announcement were for his benefit. "He hasn't been here in a long time. Quite a troublemaker, that one. What's he want, Cyrus?"

"He is my brother. He comes for a visit," said Cyrus flatly, his face closed, his eyes resting coldly on Jackson's.

"All right, all right! Just so he don't stir up trouble. Mighty nice party, Cyrus." Jackson moved away toward the food.

Jules and Cyrus stood silent, as though they were alone in an empty space. For Jules, this blow came suddenly. He could not speak. He waited, hoping Cyrus would say, "He comes only for a visit with us. That is all." But as the silence between them lengthened, Jules knew the time he foolishly had thought would never come had, after all, arrived. He stared across the room, seeing nothing, his face set.

Cyrus shifted uneasily. Jackson was right in suspecting Wenonga's motives. Wenonga was a shaman. He never traveled without a purpose. That his purpose this time involved a friend, Jules, to whom Cyrus owed his son's life, was cause for sorrow. "He said he comes to see you, that he has business with you."

"Then," said Jules quietly, turning away, "I will expect him." He searched for his daughter. Quayo he saw in the lean-to, but not Supaya or Jacques. He found them outside with a large group gathered around the fire, popping corn. Jacques had said something amusing, and they all laughed. Supaya and Kineu were standing together, shoulders touching. Jules watched them, studying his daughter's face. Her wide brow and high cheekbones were softened by youth and spoke of a strength yet to be realized. But her eyes, large and slanted like his own, and her full, generous mouth spoke of a ready capacity for passion. That was clear enough to Jules, seeing the unconscious but ardent yearning in her face as she looked up at Kineu, with a look that matched Kineu's own. From the depth of his own worn years, Jules wondered bitterly what kept them apart.

Someone in front of Jules spoke. Supaya turned her head and saw her father, standing outside the circle, watching her. He met her eyes, not casually but keenly, as if he would tell her something, holding her eyes with his own, the corners of his mouth turned in a rueful smile that was unfamiliar and disturbing to Supaya. Standing there beyond the firelight in the dusk of evening, he seemed to recede from her, to become a stranger. A sudden fear struck her, and she almost called out to him above the others' voices, but then she saw that he was gone. She shivered with apprehension. That he intended a meaning she was certain. But what? Feeling lost and uneasy, she turned back to Kineu.

Before the half moon rose, everyone had gone. Jules had found Rhea waiting in the house. Unsmiling, he studied her, a glint of suppressed anger in his eye, which she, in her pleasure at his seeking her out, misunderstood. When he inclined his head and walked out the door, she rose and followed him.

Jacques walked home with Maud and her family. Quayo, not finding Jules, called Supaya. They gathered up Jules' gifts and walked home, Kineu accompanying them.

"Where is Father, Grandma?"

Quayo was evasive. "Talking, smoking." She was too weary to be bothered. Her old legs ached from standing. She thought only of her bed, downstairs to save her climbing the ladderlike stairs. When they reached home, Quayo, mumbling to herself, went in at once, leaving Supaya and Kineu alone.

"Something is wrong," insisted Supaya.

"Why? What could be wrong?"

"Didn't you see him? The way he looked when we were standing by the fire?"

Kineu laughed softly. "I saw only you. Come," putting his arm around her waist. "Let's walk under the trees."

"He was telling me something, Kineu, I know it. Then he was gone. It was like a bad omen."

Kineu drew her into the shadow of the woods. Behind them, moonlight whitened the ridged, barren garden and shone frostily on the roof of the house, whose black shadow fell aslant the ground. On the whitened road lay the black, pointed shadows of pines.

"You see," whispered Kineu, drawing her round so she faced him, "it was a good omen. We are here, together."

"But Kineu, I think . . ."

He suddenly put both arms around her, pressing her so close that her breath came in a little gasp. "Think of me, Suppy!"

"Ah, but I do," Supaya whispered, forgetting her worry. "I think of you all the time." She relaxed against him, delighting in his tight embrace. She put her arms around his neck and he bent his head and kissed her gently, soft lip against lip. He kissed her cheeks and the curve of her neck.

"Suppy, Suppy," he whispered, holding her so tight she could scarcely breathe. She stroked his hair, passed her fingertips tenderly over his brow, traced the long, thin scar that he had gotten defending her. And as she had yearned to do, she caressed the line of his cheek and jaw and let her fingers linger on the curve of his mouth. They kissed again, and then, through the stifled beating of their hearts, they heard a sound.

Kineu raised his head. Listening, they heard not footsteps but a low, happy humming. "It's Jacques, coming home. Oh, Kineu, I must go in. Father might come! No, Kineu, please!" She braced her hands against his chest. "I must go."

They waited to be sure Jacques was in his room; then, after a last, lingering kiss and a slow parting of hands, Supaya ran to the door and let herself in.

Much, much later, when the moon had sunk below the still, black waters of the lake, and the road, like a tunnel, held only darkness, Jules came home. He hesitated briefly before opening the door, then moved soundlessly across the room. Supaya, blissfully asleep in the loft, never heard him, nor did Jacques. Quayo, muttering and twitching in the restless half-sleep of the old, mistook the figure that paused by her bed for the spirit of her father and dropped off to another dream of childhood.

The sun rose like a fiery, angry eye, then disappeared behind slate-black clouds that rolled slowly out of the west, bringing the first snow of winter.

Jacques lit the oil lamp, and Quayo set out cups of steaming tea, placing one before Jules, who seemed not to see it. Since rising, he had scarcely spoken, but sat facing the door, one arm resting on the table. Almost, thought Quayo, watching him uneasily, as though he were expecting someone. But she didn't question him, for there was that in his face that brought back the dreadful memory of the day her daughter Shooskonee, his wife, had died. Remembering, Quayo rested her hand lightly on his shoulder.

Supaya had just come downstairs when there was a knock on the door. Quayo and Jacques turned. Jules didn't move.

"I'll go," said Supaya. She opened the door and stepped back as a gust of cold air and a few whirling snowflakes blew in.

Wenonga stood on the doorstep.

CHAPTER FIVE

Standing in the blowing snow, Wenonga waited to be invited in. Snow clung to his shaggy hair and lay on his broad, blanketed shoulders. The wind buffeted against him, blew his hair across his face, but he stood massive and solid as a tree rooted in the earth. In the one startled moment between Supaya's opening the door and Quayo's coming to greet him, his large, bulging eyes took in everything—Supaya, the room beyond, Quayo and Jacques, both turned in surprise, Jules, not surprised, facing him across the table.

It was Quayo who came forward first to greet him. "*Ahnee,* Wenonga, *ahnee*! Please come in! Welcome to our home!"

He entered with a deliberate, stately step, following Quayo, who graciously offered him a chair by the fireplace. He flung off his blanket and settled himself, leaning slightly forward, his head resting between his thick, hunched shoulders.

Jules greeted him stiffly, then formally presented his son, Jacques, and his daughter, Supaya.

Wenonga looked back and forth at them all, moving only his eyes, looking from one to the other in the suspicious manner of a guest who knows that wherever he goes, he is more respected than liked, more feared than welcomed.

Supaya had never seen such eyes as his, large, red-veined, reddened even at the rims as if a fire burned inside him. They were powerful, compelling, and they lingered on her as though without raising a hand he would grasp her, hold her, penetrate her thoughts. She knew this was the shaman who had saved her mother's life when she gave birth to Jacques. Quayo had told them many times of the powerful shaman. Supaya had imagined him as an awesome but beneficent figure. Now she found him both repelling and fascinating, also frightening, and when Quayo sent her on the run to Neegonas for an extra pot and to the root cellar for vegetables, she went at once, glad to be out of his sight.

While Quayo and Supaya worked to prepare a meal of the best they had, Jules and Wenonga exchanged gifts of tobacco, and lit their pipes. They puffed in silence for a time. Then Wenonga spoke.

"I hear you healed my brother's son. That is well. They are grateful."

"I am happy that I was able to cure him."

"I lost my first son," said Wenonga, reminding Jules of what he already knew. "He was taken from me by a man jealous of my blessings. But I was revenged. He paid for his spite." Remembering, Wenonga frowned and glared at the fire, his eyes reflecting its red blaze. Jules and Jacques were cautiously silent. A shaman's retribution was fearful. Any discussion could bring it much too close

Quayo brought the men hot tea, and as they drank, Jules turned the conversation to more general matters, inquiring about a cousin of his who the year before had transferred to the Two Bluffs Reserve where Wenonga lived, far away.

While the venison, onions, and potatoes simmered, filling the room with their aroma, Quayo and Supaya made berry pies and scone. Whenever Supaya turned or raised her head, she caught Wenonga's glance following her. She was disturbed, and would have spoken of it to Quayo, but Quayo, delighted to honor Wenonga, the man who had once saved her daughter's life, was oblivious to Supaya's uneasiness, intent only on serving every good thing she could, even the prized white cheese curds a friend had given her.

When the meal was ready, the men sat at the table, and Quayo and Supaya served them. Wenonga ate rapidly, gulping his food, glancing suspiciously at the others while he chewed. Jules scarcely touched his food, eating only enough to avoid being rude. Quayo, puzzled by Jules' lack of warmth, worked all the harder at making Wenonga welcome, urging him to eat more and more. Supaya hung back, staying behind Wenonga when she could, longing to be free to go and meet Kineu as she had promised the night before.

Finally Wenonga finished. He relit his pipe and tried to shape his deep, rough voice to friendly tones. "I see your younger daughter is a handsome young woman now. I see too that she wears a necklace of power." He smiled widely at Supaya, but to her it was as if a wild animal had bared its teeth, and she dropped her eyes, unable to respond. Addressing Jules, he said, "I have heard much about her from my relatives. I hear she is well-trained in our ways. Like her mother," he paused, emphasizing the word "mother," "she is a fine cook and a hard worker."

Quayo was pleased and began to praise Supaya's skills, but Jules interrupted coldly. "Quayo, bring more tea."

"Ah," said Wenonga, as Supaya placed the maple syrup near his cup. "Then she must have clever hands." He reached out suddenly with his broad, thick fingers to take her hand. But Supaya snatched her hand away and moved around to the other side of the table.

Wenonga said politely, "I have also heard good things about your son." But his eyes were on Supaya as he spoke.

"He is a dutiful son," said Jules shortly.

"As you know," said Wenonga, staring now at Jules, who sat with lowered eyes, "I have a second son.

When his mother was taken from us, the agent sent him away to government boarding school for a long time. He learned many things there. Now he has returned home." He paused, drew on his pipe, then said, "It is time now for your payment."

Jules might not have heard, might have been struck by misfortune and sitting by himself, he was so pensive and silent. His voice seemed to have died within him. Quayo looked from one to the other, startled by Wenonga's unexpected claim of a payment and disturbed by Jules' silence. Jacques, sensitive to the growing tension, was puzzled and uneasy. He saw Wenonga's increasing impatience for an answer, his burning eyes fixed on his father, and he unconsciously braced himself for a spring. Supaya, wanting only to be gone, moved restlessly, and as she did so, her father spoke. His words were brittle as ice.

"I have not forgotten my debt. But I am not prepared to pay so soon."

Wenonga glared. The corners of his mouth turned down in fierce displeasure. "But I was prepared to cure your wife. And I have waited many years for payment. I will not be cheated." Scraping back his chair, he rose ponderously, His polite words thinly masked the anger emanating from him. "It was good to smoke a pipe with you. I will go now." He wrapped himself in his blanket and strode to the door, where he paused, and ignoring everyone except Jules, said, "I will expect your promised payment before I return home."

As soon as the door closed behind Wenonga, Joe Crow swooped down from a rafter where he had been huddling in the shadows. He stepped nervously back and forth on his lame leg, squawking and ruffling his feathers. As the others watched, stunned and frightened by Wenonga's anger, Jules clicked his tongue, and the bird flew to his knee. Gently Jules stroked Joe Crow's feathers and murmured to him. Gradually the bird grew calm, then hopped onto his shoulder, nestled close, and blinked his eyes.

Unable to wait any longer, Supaya edged over to Quayo. "Grandma," she whispered, "I am going out now."

"Go," said Quayo. "Your father and I must talk."

Her coat buttoned up, her shawl wrapped snugly around her head and shoulders, Supaya took a path through the woods to West Creek. Overhead bare branches creaked in the wind. The earth was stone hard, and covered now with a layer of snow. West Creek was flowing fast, swirling over the stones, its water a cold, dull gray. Following the creek to where it emptied into the lake. Supaya saw Kineu near the water's edge, skipping stones out over the breaking waves. Thinking to surprise him, Supaya came up behind him and reached out her hands to cover his eyes. But as they encircled his head, he caught them and turned around.

She pouted. "How did you know!"

"How?" He laughed down at her, his dark eyes shining, his face ruddy from the sharp lake wind. "You made as much noise as a doe crashing through the bushes."

"Oh!" She tried to look indignant, failed, then clasped her arms about his neck and pressed her lips eagerly to his. Oblivious to the growing storm, they held each other tight, their cheeks burning cold, until a crashing wave flung its spume around them. Hands clasped, they ran up the narrow beach and into the shelter of the woods. In a grove of pines, they found a fallen log, and sitting close together, his arm tight around her, their faces touching, they made plans, their voices carried away by the wind that rocked the pine branches and scudded heavy clouds across the dark afternoon sky.

"Suppy, you know that meadow beyond the ridge

behind your father's place? It wouldn't need much clearing. We could have a house and garden. There's a good stand of trees for a windbreak. I think the Council would let me have it. I could start building now. Maybe Jacques would help me."

Supaya pictured it at once: the high, sheltered meadow, a small log house, maybe a few apple trees. Her eyes glowed. "I'll plant the garden and you can dig a root cellar and build a barn!"

"I already have my own boat and net, and I can buy my own traps." Gazing at her face so close to his, his voice trailed off. "Oh, Suppy," he whispered, "I want you now!" And for a time they forgot their plans, lost in their delight with each other. They might have met for the first time the night before, have come to truly know each other only now when every kiss, every caress seemed a revelation. The soft fullness of her breast, the curve of her body were realities beyond what he'd imagined. The touch of his hand on her flesh, the press of his body against hers made her forget everything but the desire she felt for him. Breathlessly, they kissed, as though their lips could scarcely bear to part, and Supaya whispered, "Soon, Kineu, soon!"

"I'll ask your father today, now, when we return. I don't want anyone else coming near you. I want everyone to know you are mine!"

"Kineu, there could never, never be anyone else." She held his head between both her hands and kissed him lingeringly, with all her soul, as a pledge, a seal, of her words.

After Supaya had left the house, Quayo, full of foreboding, pulled her shawl about her and, sitting down, faced Jules. "What," she asked, "did you promise Wenonga?"

Her question hung in the air. As if to shake off its weight, Jules rose, disturbing Joe Crow, who squawked a drowsy protest and flew up to a beam. Jules thrust a piece of wood into the fire and, leaning one hand against the mantel, stood looking down at the flurry of sparks. His back to Quayo and Jacques, he said, "I promised him Neegonas as wife for his son."

"But his son died," said Jacques, "as he told us."

"I knew his son died," answered Jules sharply. "That is why Neegonas could marry James. But his son's death did not wipe out my debt. As I had another daughter, so he had another son. As he told us," he added, in an angry, mimicking voice. Then he turned to face them and saw their sudden shock of understanding.

"You promised him Supaya!" exclaimed Quayo.

"I promised him Neegonas! *That* is what I said! I couldn't know he would have another son!" They stared at each other for a long moment—he trapped and furious; she accusing. Then thrusting his face toward her, he spit out his words. "Damn you, old woman! It was *your* daughter's life I paid for!"

At that Quayo dropped her eyes and turned her head aside.

Jacques looked from one to the other incredulously. "You can't!" he burst out. "You can't give her away to that man's son! I am her brother, and I say . . ."

Jules took one step, grabbed him by his shirt front and shook him. "Never dare tell me what I can or cannot do! I made a promise! You understand? It means my life! The lives of your grandmother, your sisters, your cousins!" He paused, pulled Jacques closer, and added with biting emphasis, "Your life!" Then he flung Jacques from him and turned away.

Only the soft breathing of the fire and the wind sighing against the house filled the silence. Then, not looking at them, Jules spoke quietly. "I would have given anything I had for Shooskonee. Anything. Supaya did not exist. Even you were not yet born. Later I learned of this second son, but he was sent away. A long time passed and he did not return. I hoped . . .

finally believed . . . he never would . . . that the debt would go unpaid."

With an effort, Quayo got to her feet and, going to Jules, laid her hand on his arm. "Son, come, sit down. Light your pipe. I will get us some tea."

Jules sat and lit his pipe, and Jacques came and sat on the floor beside him, head bowed. "Father," he said finally, hesitatingly, "Supaya and Kineu . . ."

Jules nodded. "I understand about Supaya and Kineu."

They were sitting toegther, drinking tea when Supaya and Kineu entered by the back door, throwing it wide and rushing in, laughing and breathless from running against the wind. Kineu latched the door and Supaya came forward smiling, drawing off her shawl and coat, her eyes sparkling.

On their way home, she had told Kineu of Wenonga's visit and his claim of a payment.

"Pay what?" Kineu had asked.

"I don't know. But I could see father was angry. Maybe you should wait and ask him about us another time."

"No. I must ask now. That has nothing to do with us. Your father will understand that."

Jules turned when they entered and watched them approach, their faces glowing from more than the cold, saw their quick, conspiratorial glances, their irrepressible smiles. In Supaya's radiant face he saw again Shooskonee and, stricken by this living memory, turned his gaze away, afraid his pain would reveal itself in his eyes. He knew Kineu would speak, and he waited.

"Uncle," said Kineu, standing at a respectful distance, "I have come to ask you for your daughter. We wish to marry." He paused, expecting Jules to smile, Jacques to leap up, Quayo to clap her hands, but all were still, their faces turned away from him. Thinking more was expected of him, he began again. "I have little, but there is land and wood for a house. I am able to hunt and . . . ."

Jules held up his hand. In that moment before her father spoke, Supaya suddenly perceived through the haze of her own happiness the tension that gripped her family. She saw Quayo turn away, and then Jacques. She recognized the forbidding lines of her father's face: the half-lowered lids, the stern set of his mouth. She was filled with dread before he spoke.

"Nephew, you have honored my daughter. But she cannot marry you. She is promised to another."

Supaya gasped. Kineu stepped back as if he'd been slapped.

"Father!" exclaimed Supaya, unbelieving. "Father, what do you mean? Promised! When was I promised? There isn't anyone else!"

"Tell her," said Quayo softly, "tell her!"

With great pain, Jules turned and met her eyes; but she saw only that his were cold and impersonal. "You will marry Wenonga's son. He came here to arrange for the marriage."

Supaya stared at him, speechless. Then, "Why?" she asked, her voice a whisper.

"I promised him a wife for his son as payment for healing your mother."

"Ayyyiii! But that was before I was born!" She rushed forward, flung herself down by his chair, and grasped his arm tightly with both hands. "Father, please, there must be some other way!" Her eyes filled with tears. "I love Kineu! I cannot leave him! I cannot leave my home and you and Grandma! I cannot marry a stranger!"

"Cannot!" repeated Jules, his eyes suddenly blazing, "cannot!" Finding relief in anger, he shook off her hands and raised his arm threateningly above her. "You will do as I say! You will remember your obligations! To me and your family! You are no longer a child! You will marry Wenonga's son!" He leaned toward her, hoping his sternness would help strengthen her. "And you will not cry!"

Her eyes fixed on him, her fist pressed against her mouth, Supaya drew back. No one moved or spoke.

"Nephew," said Jules, "you are close to our heart. You will always be welcome in our home."

Kineu was too stunned to move or speak. In his blanched face, his scar stood out as a thin white welt. He stared at Supaya as if he saw her receding from him.

Jacques took Kineu by the arm. "Come," he said quietly. "You should go. I will go with you."

When the door closed behind them, Supaya, without a word, climbed the stairs to the loft. Later, when Quayo called her, she did not answer nor did she come down. By night the sky had cleared, but the wind blew with increased fury, churning the lake into heavy waves that arced high and crashed on the beach. Unable to sleep, Jules listened to the wind beating against the house, moaning in the chimney. He heard the restless mutterings of his son and a faint movement in the loft above him that told him his daughter also was awake.

Supaya knelt in the cold by the small window at the foot of her bed, looking out at the stars that glittered like ice. She cupped the stone bear against her cheek and whispered to it. "Grandfather Mukwah, help me! I cannot help myself. Soften my father's heart! Don't let him send me away from Kineu, from my home!" She had cried until there were no more tears. Lying with her head against the sill, she gazed out at the stars swinging across the sky until her eyelids closed of their own accord and she slept, the stone bear cradled in her hand beside her cheek.

The next day Hettie appeared at their back door. She came in rubbing her cold hands together, her cheeks pink, her large, humorous face almost comically mournful. She had come, she said, for a cup of tea and to report on Aunt Theresa, who was dying.

"She refuses to leave her house," said Hettie, warming her hands round her cup. "Cousin Minnie visits her and keeps her fire going."

Quayo nodded. "She wants to die in her own place."

Neither woman mentioned Jules, who had gone out early, saying he had to check his traps. Nor did Hettie speak of Kineu, who had come home with Jacques, then left by himself and had still not returned. Jacques had explained what had happened to his aunt, and now her moist eyes rested sadly on Supaya, who sat apart, saying nothing, her head bent over her work.

Supaya had come down only after Jules left. Eyes downcast, face full of grief, she moved as if in a trance, numb to those about her. Quayo and Jacques had watched her with concern. Now, Quayo and Hettie spoke aloud of daily matters, but their eyes said to each other: It is great cause for sadness. It is painful. We must give her time.

Supaya, weaving quills into the round lid of a birchbark box, clung to her work as the only stable thing in her shattered world. Automatically she made the regularly spaced holes with her awl, then poked the quill up through the lid, flattened it with her thumbnail, poked it down through another hole and pulled it taut. She scarcely saw the work she did, nor did she think of Kineu, or of leaving her home and going with Wenonga, but only of her father, stern and forbidding. She heard his words, over and over again until, feeling smothered, she abruptly thrust her work aside, and passing Quayo and Hettie without a glance, left the house.

The furious wind of the night before had stilled. Low clouds covered the sky like a soft, gray blanket. Occasional snowflakes drifted down. The air was cold but not bitter, and Supaya lifted her face and breathed in deeply. She walked aimlessly, through the woods and along the ridge toward the spring. Her father's words no longer sounded in her ears. Her mind was blessedly empty. She was conscious only of the woods, of its spare, winter beauty, with yesterday's snow drifted along the path and in the hollows. Following a barely discernible trail, she came to a large dead branch blown down by the wind. Lifting it aside, she saw pressed in the light powder of snow the print of a huge paw. Grandfather Mukwah! Startled, she looked about, but saw only leafless underbrush, rocks and trees, birch, cedar and fir, some split by the night's wind, their raw inner wood exposed. Cautiously, alert for any sound, Supaya walked on. Reaching the spring, she stopped to listen to its soft, steady murmur. A constant promise of life, it welled up from within the earth and rippled outward, crystal clear above the muddy bottom. On impulse, Supaya knelt down, thrust her cupped hand into the water, and lifted it to her mouth. Icy cold, it pained her hand and numbed her lips, but she drank eagerly, again and again, exhilarated by the chill that shocked her body, waking her senses and reviving her mind. Her vision cleared as if she had awakened from a nightmare and was grateful to find herself on solid ground. Curling her painfully throbbing hand inside her pocket, she started home. Her Grandfather had given her strength, had shown her the path she must follow. She would speak to her father again, this time quietly, calmly.

It was dusk when Jules returned and hung his catch from a tree for the night. Supaya was waiting for him, and when he stood by the fire warming himself, she came and stood beside him.

"Father, I must speak to you about my . . . my marriage." Jules inclined his head. "It is true? I must marry Wenonga's son? There is no other safe way?"

"No other way. If there were," and now he turned to look intently at her, "I would have taken it."

She kept her eyes steady and her mouth firm. "When must it be?"

"Tomorrow Wenonga comes and we will speak to the agent about your transferring to another band. Wenonga returns to his reserve on the next day's boat."

Calmly, Supaya said, "I cannot leave that soon. I will not be ready. I must gather my things."

Jules studied his daughter's profile, the high forehead and strong chin, the proud, haughty pose of her head, with gratification. He answered gravely, respecting her newly realized self-containment. "I will speak to Wenonga. We will arrange it for next spring."

"Thank you, Father," said Supaya and she turned away to help Quayo.

Watching her from a great and increasing distance, Jules pondered the possibility of their ever meeting again in loving trust as father and child. Suddenly, he felt unusually weary from his day's hunting. He lit his pipe and sat down before the fire, soberly contemplating the lonely ridge of his life.

CHAPTER SIX

It was Hettie who came with news of Aunt Theresa's death, her volatile nature changing from sadness over Supaya to breathless fright over the revelation of Aunt Theresa as a witch. She repeated Minnie's account, relayed through three others and embellished with her own sense of the dramatic. "She was lying still, breathing her last." Hettie demonstrated, holding her breath, shutting her eyes, and letting her mouth hang. "Suddenly," popping her eyes wide open and half rising from her chair, "she sat straight up and invited them in—the spirits! She called them by name!" adding, to forestall any questions, "Minnie would not repeat them. Then she insisted Minnie serve them tea!" She leaned forward, her voice hushed. "But Minnie sprinkled wild ginger on the fire when Theresa wasn't looking!"

"Maybe, but I don't believe it," said Quayo flatly.

"But it's true!" cried Hettie, wanting to believe. "She was trying to get up and come to the table with them when she died! Minnie had to stop her!"

Quayo shrugged.

"And when Minnie left the house, she saw a dog running off into the woods!"

"There are always dogs about," said Quayo.

Hettie's large mouth closed in a disappointed pout. She turned toward her brother Jules, hoping for his support, when there was a knock on the door.

Jules, who was shaping a leg for a new chair, put

down his work. Giving Supaya a warning glance, he
went to the door and opened it wide.

Wenonga entered with a blast of cold air that made
the fire swoop up the chimney. Hettie rose instantly.
Tales of witches were one thing, Wenonga quite another. She murmured to Quayo and left hurriedly.

Wenonga sat again in Jules' chair, and though he
acknowledged their greetings, his expression was thun-
derous, his eyes fiery, ready to blaze in anger. Jules,
cool and self-possessed, offered him tobacco and fire
for his pipe and said smoothly, "We will have tea before we go to see the agent," thus informing Wenonga
of his intention to fulfill his obligation without quarrel.

Visibly surprised, Wenonga settled back. His tension relaxed but his suspicion increased. He stared at
Jules, then at Supaya, searching their faces for trick-
ery. Having readied herself, Supaya withstood his gaze
coolly.

"We will arrange for the transfer now," said Jules,
"so the matter will be settled but my daughter cannot
leave her home with you tomorrow." He saw Wenonga's face tighten, his eyes flash, and he continued
calmly. "It is too soon, too unexpected for her to
be ready."

Supaya had been watching Wenonga and now, to
their surprise as well as her own, since she had not
anticipated speaking at all, she found herself saying
haughtily, "I must prepare for such a journey. I have
many things to gather." She spoke directly to Wenonga, flinging the words down like a challenge.

Wenonga turned and considered her, taking a long
draw on his pipe to cover his surprise at this young
woman who apparently was no longer afraid of him.
He glanced back at Jules, whose impassive face hid
the great pride he took in his daughter.

"She will be prepared to go with you when the lake
opens in the spring," said Jules after an interval of
silence.

Feeling obscurely at a disadvantage but unable to find an objection, Wenonga agreed. "That is well. I will come on the first boat in the spring." Then he added, not to be outdone in the matter of pride. "We, too, must prepare."

The wind was rising, whirling the snow falling from a distant, uniformly gray sky. Jules and Wenonga walked ahead, their footprints leaving faint outlines, Supaya following behind.

Jackson lived in the house built for the agent by the Indians. The largest, finest house on the reserve, it had two stories and a roofed verandah across the front and along both sides. One of the two spacious front rooms opening off the center hall served as office. Jackson's elderly housekeeper opened the door. She was gray-haired and always wore an apron as if her entire life were lived in the kitchen. In answer to Jules' request to see Mr. Jackson, she stepped back, opened the office door, and pointed. She never spoke to Indians, whom she saw as children—dangerous, unpredictable children. The silence she maintained was her only protective barrier. Jules and Supaya she knew by sight, but not Wenonga. Wrapped in his blanket, he filled the hallway like a huge, half-tame animal. The housekeeper stood aside as they filed into the office, then hurriedly shut the door.

Jackson, in vest and shirt sleeves, sat at his desk, his back to the bare windows, his balding head bent over a ledger. Except for several straight chairs lined against the wall and a framed print of the new king, Edward VII, the room was empty. A small iron stove in one corner radiated a slight warmth. Jackson seldom invited any Indian to sit down, believing it bad policy to allow them to feel too familiar, especially outspoken ones like Jules Cedar. He let them stand and wait while he finished a row of figures.

"Well, Jules," said Jackson, finally looking up at the two men. "I see you've come calling with a visitor.

And . . ." he tilted his head to one side, ". . . your very pretty daughter."

"Mr. Jackson," said Jules, in the careful, distinct voice he used when dealing with a social inferior, "this is Wenonga Red Sky, from the Two Bluffs Reserve."

"Oh yes. I heard you were coming." His flat tone suggested Wenonga might better have stayed home. He leaned back in his chair. "Well, boys, what can I do for you?"

A flicker of amused contempt at this man's bad manners crossed Jules' face, an expression Jackson misread as simple friendliness. "My daughter, Supaya, is to marry Wenonga Red Sky's son in the spring. She needs a paper of transfer from this band roll to his."

"Well! Getting married, is she!" He looked again at Supaya. "Mmmn. How old is she?" he asked. "Fifteen? Eighteen?" Jules raised his eyebrows slightly, appeared not to understand. Jackson glanced again at Supaya. "Oh well," he said, half to himself, "I can look it up in the birth records. Probably none too soon anyway. Here, let me get the facts down. Sophia Cedar, daughter of Jules Cedar, will marry . . ." he glanced up at Wenonga, waiting for him to supply the name.

"She will marry Eli Red Sky," growled Wenonga.

"Eli Red Sky," repeated Jackson, writing. "Marriage to take place here or there?"

"There," said Jules.

"There. In the spring, you said?"

"Yes."

"All right," said Jackson. "I'll write you out a paper of transfer." He scribbled on a small sheet of paper. Silently they waited. When he finished, he held the paper up, uncertain which man should have it.

Again surprised at her own audacity, Supaya stepped forward. "I will take it." As startled as if a carved figure had spoken, Jackson hesitated and looked inquiringly at the men. "It is *my* transfer," insisted Supaya.

"*I* will keep it." Imperiously she held out her hand.

Seeing neither Jules nor Wenonga so much as flick an eyelash, Jackson grudgingly handed her the paper.

"I can even read it," said Supaya tartly. She folded the paper and put it in her leather pouch. Then she turned toward the door, paused, and looked back impatiently at the two men as if to ask what they waited for.

Jules' eyes crinkled with amused understanding. Her anger, he saw, was deep and strong, unexpected even to herself. Such anger was good. It gave her strength.

"Thank you, Mr. Jackson," he said gravely, and they filed out of the office.

Later, when she was alone, Supaya took out the paper and read it, saying the words softly to herself.

Agent Gerald Toomis
Two Bluffs Reserve
Ontario, Canada

Sophia Cedar has contracted to marry Eli Red Sky. This marriage is to take place on your reserve and her name has to be removed from my band roll for Indians on this island. Please write Ottawa when this marriage has taken place and have them place her name on your band roll.

S. M. Jackson, Agent
Stone Island Reserve
Ontario, Canada

Refolding it, Supaya pondered the name—Eli Red Sky. She could form no impression from the name. She dreaded to think the son might resemble the father. But that name would become her name, and she would bear it with dignity. Meanwhile, she had until spring. She put the paper back into her pouch, wishing the winter might never end.

* * *

A wake was held for Aunt Theresa, the body laid out in Hettie's house since her husband, Arthur, was Theresa's nephew and her only living relative. Reverend Harris came to pray over the old lady whom he had once visited on her tiny island years before when he was newly arrived at Stone Island and wanted to introduce himself to all those parishioners living on several smaller islands included in the reserve. It was a visit he had never repeated. Theresa had been happy to see him, offered him tea and scone, and nodded encouragingly when he spoke, his voice straining uncomfortably to pierce through her deafness. At parting he had given her a small card with a verse from the Bible printed on it; whereupon, searching through a box, she had found a carved bone amulet which she had pressed upon him, smiling sweetly and instructing him that he should carry it always as protection against the water spirits. Now he murmured prayers above the shrunken old body while her nephew and friends solemnly watched.

After his departure everyone relaxed, and the wake took on a party air. Food and drink were served, and the older people present told humorous stories of Aunt Theresa's past, when her fierce independence combined with her deafness—which they exaggerated to a phenomenal degree—resulted in hilarious misunderstandings. Relishing such stories of the past, the watchers celebrated Aunt Theresa throughout the long night. With the coming of dawn, small items were brought forward and gently laid in the open coffin: her best needle, her favorite tea cup, and a new pair of moccasins to last her on her journey to the next world. Then the oldest man present, whose memories included a young, aggressively flirtatious Theresa, addressed her on behalf of them all. "Theresa, it is time for you to go. May these things we give help you on your journey. Our thoughts go with you. Soon we will follow in your path." Then the watchers dispersed, walking home in the pale dawn.

At midday Reverend Harris conducted the church service. The Cedars sat in the back row as they always did on those rare occasions when they attended church. Supaya could see Neegonas and James and their two small children sitting near the front, and two rows behind were Aunt Hettie and her family, Kineu at the end of the row. Supaya had not seen him since he had left the house with Jacques three days earlier.

Only three days, yet during that time her life had been severely wrenched. Her world was no longer secure, but uncertain and frightening. She saw now that one must do what was necessary, struggle to secure what blessings one could, and depend, finally, on them and oneself. Only one's guardian was forever constant and unchanging. This perception so abruptly forced upon her was revealing a strength of resolve and a capacity for action she hadn't realized she possessed. Even now she did not fully recognize her own capabilities, but reacted from moment to moment out of shock and anger at what seemed to her to have been a long deception. Gazing at the back of Kineu's head, she knew only that she wanted him, that she needed to take something, someone for her own. Sitting on the church bench, her face hooded by her shawl, she didn't hear the preacher's words or join in the singing. She was remembering the pressure of Kineu's mouth on hers, the touch of his hands, and her whole body ached for him.

She rose automatically with the others as the congregation filed out of the church and followed the coffin to the nearby cemetery. The Christian burial demanded by the church was carried out with difficulty; two men had worked for hours with pick and shovel to gouge a grave out of the frozen earth. Reverend Harris stood at the gravehead and the people gathered round as the coffin was lowered.

Across the backs of those lowering the coffin, Supaya saw Kineu, standing at the far edge of the group, looking directly at her. His face, always alight with energy and purpose, was drawn and sad, his eyes dull. Seeing him so was painful, yet she could not look away from him. The preacher spoke a prayer, then everyone joined in singing a hymn, their vigorous voices resounding in the cold air, reasserting life in the midst of the gray, cold cemetery with its white wooden crosses.

As the two diggers began shoveling back the raw earth, Supaya knew what she would do. Turning, she slipped through the crowd of singers. Once beyond them, she stopped, looked back at Kineu, then walked swiftly away.

Kineu allowed her a few minutes' start, then followed. When he saw she was heading toward the beach where Jacques had a small fishing shack and grounded his rowboat, Kineu turned aside and headed for his own boat.

The lake was frozen along the shoreline in grotesque, humped, and windblown shapes, forming in places conical ice volcanoes that spouted water. Beyond, ice floated in patches, lifting and falling with the rhythm of the greenish-gray water. Boats could still push their way through, their bows protected with metal plates, but soon the lake would be frozen across. Then it would be possible to walk to Aunt Theresa's little island, and men would begin fishing through holes in the ice.

Getting Jacques' boat to open water was difficult. Supaya dragged and pushed and pulled, slipping on the ice, wetting her feet and skirts. Finally she pushed it into the water. She rowed strongly, bending low and pulling the oars forward through floating ice. When she was more than halfway across, she saw coming from the far shoreline another boat, small and dark in the distance, with a solitary rower. She rowed past the point that sheltered the cove in front of Aunt Theresa's house. When she could go no further against the ice, she got out and hauled the boat across the rough, frozen ice up onto the beach. The snow that had been drifting down for several days was now falling heavily, a fine, swirling snow that was rapidly covering the ground, blending the lake with the shore.

Obscured by the snow and dwarfed by the dark woods looming behind it, the unpainted frame house looked even smaller than Supaya remembered. No light shone from its window, no smoke rose from the stack. Minnie's insistence that Aunt Theresa had been a witch had effectively frightened off any neighbor who might otherwise have been glad to move into an empty house. Supaya went around to the back door and found that Minnie had stockpiled a good supply of wood. She carried several armloads inside the lean-to before latching the door against the blowing snow.

Aunt Theresa's one-room home was, as her life had been, reduced to essentials: floor, walls, table, all were bare. No curtain hung at the one small window, no clothes from the wall pegs. Even the rope bed retained no impression of her frail body. Only the worn pad on the rocker seat and four untouched cups of cold tea gave any indication that she had lived there. Even so, and wet and chilled though she was, Supaya felt at home. She and Kineu had spent many afternoons with Aunt Theresa, had brought her supplies, climbed her apple trees, picked beans and squash for her, and played along the beach in front of her house. From Pine Point Supaya had often gazed across the water at the hill where she had dreamed, and it was there that Kineu had found her stone bear. All these memories filled Aunt Theresa's bare house with warmth; only she herself, who had invested her home with a serenity of spirit, was missing.

Supaya shook the snow from her shawl and hung it on a peg. She got down an old oil lamp from the shelves in the lean-to, lit it, and placed it in the middle of the table, being careful not to disturb the tea cups. She was making up the fire in the stove when the front door opened and Kineu entered, covered with snow and panting from his run up the beach. He leaned against the door and stared at her a moment.

Then he said, "I could see the light from the shore. Even through the snow."

"I am glad," said Supaya. She approached him and put out her hand; then, suddenly shy before his questioning look, drew it back. "Your coat and feet are wet."

"So are yours."

She averted her eyes and turned toward the stove. "I have made up the fire. It should be warm soon."

"Suppy, what . . . why have we come here?"

A flash of impatience that he should have to ask made her answer petulant. "Because I wanted to! And I'm going to stay as long as I please!" In a softer tone, her face hidden by her hair hanging loose for Aunt Theresa's funeral, she added, "We can stay here if we want. No one will mind. I am free to do as I like until the lake boat returns in the spring. "That is," she raised her head to look at him, "if you want to."

"Want to!" His face was suddenly alive. "Want to!" He gripped her shoulders, then caught her close in a tight hug and rubbed his cheek against hers. "I thought . . . I thought we'd never be together again!" They laughed together at this absurdity. He put his forehead against hers and gazed into her eyes with such an intensity of meaning that she caught her breath and pulled away.

"Let's see if there's any food left."

Reluctantly, he let her go and they began searching through tins and old birchbark boxes. They found half a can of tea, dried meat and fish, dried peas, dried apples, and two pieces of rock-hard scone. But before she could prepare food for themselves, Supaya had to make an offering.

She took some meat, apples, and bread to the stove and, lifting off one lid, put the food into the flames. As it spit and crackled and the smoke curled upward, Supaya murmured, "We thank you, Aunt Theresa, for the use of your home and your possessions. Enjoy this food. May it give you strength for your journey. We will remember you always." Only after the food had burned and the smoke had faded away did Supaya put on a pot of soup for themselves and feel free to clear away the four cups of stale tea. Kineu climbed the ladder and rummaged about in the loft.

"What is up there?" asked Supaya.

"Field mice," answered Kineu with a laugh. "And some old covers. Come and see."

Supaya climbed up until she could see over the edge of the loft. "Covers? We could use them."

"And there is an old trunk back in the corner. Shall I open it?"

"No. No, don't," said Supaya, descending the ladder. "We shouldn't disturb her things. Just bring the covers."

"The mice will be cold," said Kineu, carrying the quilts down.

"Let them climb in with us then," said Supaya airily, turning back to the stove. But Kineu's arms slid around her from behind; he nuzzled his face in the curve of her neck. "Suppy," he whispered, "you should take off your wet clothes."

"But the soup . . ." she protested weakly.

"I don't want any soup," he murmured, kissing the back of her neck where her hair fell apart. "I want you."

She turned in his arms, held his face between her hands. "All right," she whispered back, brushing his lips with her own. "Let me go then."

He watched as she smoothed Aunt Theresa's bed, spreading over it the covers from the loft. Then she turned down the oil lamp until it was only a soft dull glow in the dark shadowy room. She removed her wet moccasins and stepped out of her damp skirts, hanging them over a chair back and laying her blouse and undershirt across the seat. Shivering, she slid quickly under the old quilts. Kineu stripped rapidly, dropping his clothes on the floor. He stood for one brief, breathless moment, poised, looking down at Supaya, her hair spread around her shoulders, the stone of her necklace resting between her breasts, the two curved bear claws stark against her skin. He saw the gleam of her eyes before they closed and her arms reached out for him. They kissed as never before, mouths opening to each other. Their legs entwined, their bodies straining to become one. Hungrily, he caressed and kissed her body until she arched, pushing up against him, her head falling back in an agony that found release only in his hard, muscular thrusting. Then her arms relaxed their grip and clasped him gently as he lay on her. Like survivors of a storm, they breathed deeply and peacefully. Heads tilted together, his arm flung across her, they drifted into sleep.

Hours later, Supaya awoke. The lamp still glowed, a soft, warm eye in the dark. She crossed the cold floor, put more wood in the stove and turned off the lamp. Sliding quickly back under the covers, she fitted herself as naturally against Kineu's sleeping form as if it had been a habit of years.

In the morning they woke simultaneously and smiled at each other. She reached up and stroked his head, caressed his shoulder, invited him with soft eyes; leaning over her, he smoothed back her hair and kissed the line of her throat and swelling breasts. This time their lovemaking was slower, more deeply satisfying, and afterwards they lay still, loathe to move, minds empty, bodies content.

Snow had fallen heavily all night and continued to fall all that day and the next. The wind had risen again, and when Kineu went out for more wood, he could scarcely see the backhouse through the snow that whipped about and blew up like a white veil in front of him. He reached elbow deep to find the wood and returned with snow thick on his clothes, his hair, coating even his eyelashes. Supaya laughed at him, circling round, retreating in pretended horror. They laughed a great deal that day. They were snowbound, cut off from the whole world, and their only concern, their only interest, was each other.

The third morning Supaya stood at the window and looked out at a white world. She had begun to feel restless, confined. She had no work to occupy her, and she imagined Quayo's and her father's concern for her, their possible need for her help. Outside, land, water, and sky had lost all boundary lines. Snow fell out of a white, luminous sky where the sun was only a pale, glowing disk, fell so thick it confined all distance to one great curve of white blending with a white earth.

"Kineu, we will have to dig out the boats." Kineu, sitting with his legs stretched out, chin on chest, didn't answer. "Kineu?"

"You want to go back, don't you," he said, stating it as fact.

Supaya turned. "We have to go back," she said gently. "Our families will think we are lost. Besides, we can't stay here all winter."

"We could," he said sharply, accusingly. "You know we could."

At his words, knowing the hurt behind them, Supaya knelt beside him and sought to take his hand. "Kineu, we can come back! We can still be together sometimes. But I must go home, I have . . ."

Kineu withdrew his hand and coldly disregarded her words. "We could even leave here and go far away. They would never find us. But you don't want to."

Dismayed, Supaya dropped her eyes, realized she was on her knees, and stood up. She felt an anger she had never expected to feel toward Kineu, for his rebuff and his suggestion that she ignore her duty, endanger her family as well as themselves. Twice now she had knelt to plead with a man. She would remember never to kneel to a man again. She had tied up her moccasins around her ankles and was putting on her coat when Kineu touched her shoulder.

"What are you going to do?"

"I am going to dig out the boat and go back."

"Suppy!" His smile, his eyes begged her forgiveness. "I will come with you. We will go back together."

Kineu took two poles from the drying rack and together they went toward the beach. The snow blew into their faces, fanned up by a steady wind that bared the icy rocks in some places, formed long, deep drifts in others. The two overturned boats were covered with high domes of snow, easily knocked off. Their spirits revived by the bracing air, they found they could laugh again. Kineu showered Supaya with snow, and she chased him into a drift, where they fell and rolled over in mock struggle. He caught her and held tight, and she collapsed against him. Panting, their faces ruddy and eyes bright, they looked searchingly at each other, then suddenly kissed, a quick, vigorous kiss of mutual forgiveness.

They headed out across the frozen lake, each dragging a boat behind and thrusting a pole through the snow ahead to test the solidity of the ice. The sun, an intense spot of light in a white sky, alternately brightened and faded as strong wind gusts lifted the snow and whirled it around in a frosty, blinding curtain. As they neared Stone Island, the mass of trees along the shore gradually emerged. They hauled the boats well up on the beach near the trees and turned them over. Kineu led the way through the woods, breaking a path for Supaya. When they came in sight of her home, he turned off and she went on alone.

No comment was made when Supaya returned. No questions were asked. Jules had seen her leave Quayo's side in the cemetery and he had seen Kineu following her minutes later. When Jacques found his boat missing, they understood where she had gone. She quietly resumed her place in the family as if she had never been away.

The storm lasted for several more days, then tapered off and the sun shone blindingly bright, casting long, bluish shadows across the glittering snow. Eagerly people emerged from their homes, and soon a network of packed snow trails appeared, connecting houses, store, church, and school.

Hettie came to visit, rolling her eyes comically at Supaya while relaying the latest gossip to Quayo. Jules strapped on snowshoes and left to check his traps set out along the meadow streams and in the rabbit runs. Jacques went fishing on the lake with Kineu, where they set up a blanket windbreak for shelter, prepared to sit for hours hunched over the lines they let down through the ice. Supaya listened amused to Hettie's conversation while she carefully cut out some of the finest birchbark to be used as lining for her quill boxes. She had finished the quillwork on several—one small box, four inches across, and two larger ones to be used as collar boxes. She hoped to sell them to Mr. Bonnet in order to buy material for dresses she would need when she left in the spring. Quayo and Hettie discussed the New Year's feast, an annual communal dinner and dance held in the Council House. This event taxed the resources of every kitchen on the reserve. The two women were planning what dishes they would prepare when Neegonas stopped by with her two small children. Quayo poured another cup of tea and gave her grandchildren some fried bread.

As she drank her tea, Neegonas studied Supaya, only half listening to the older women. Finally she said, "I hear you will be leaving in the spring to get married." Supaya glanced up and nodded. "Of course, some girls will go with a man without being married. Or so I hear," she added in an insinuating tone.

There was a pause in both conversations. Supaya smiled at her sister. "And some girls," she said, "get married only because they get caught with a baby."

"Neegonas," said Quayo sharply, "what do you plan to bring for the feast?"

Neegonas shrugged. "Corn soup. Maybe a stew . . . bread." She wondered why she had bothered to ocme and soon left, giving her older son an unnecessary shove out the door.

"Miss Harris is teaching the children a song for the feast program," said Hettie. "Are you helping this year, Suppy?"

"No, Aunt Hettie, I'm too busy. You said you had an embroidery pattern you would give me. Could you show me now?"

Hettie did so and suggested that Alexandria, an old woman who lived on the far side of the reserve and whose eyesight was now too poor for her to do any embroidery, had several good patterns she might give in exchange for food.

Supaya, planning seriously for her new life, was eager for every pattern, every recipe, every medicine she could get. She was determined to be a good wife and not shame her family. She began visiting many of the older women on the reserve, exchanging beadwork, moccasins, or food for bits of their knowledge and skill. Often Kineu accompanied her and they would have an hour or two alone together.

When they visited Auntie Em to bring her food and

keep up her fire, her old eyes sparkled at sight of
Kineu.

"Ah, ah, you have come with your young man,"
she said to Supaya. "I know," nodding her head wisely,
"you want to be alone. Up to the loft, go on! That's
what we used to do. I remember well. But now I am
tired. I will go to sleep." She promptly shut her eyes,
pretending. After Supaya put the pot of stew on the
stove and the pie Quayo had sent on the table beside
her, she and Kineu climbed the stairs to the loft. Then
Auntie Em's eyes opened and she rocked contentedly,
smiling to herself, waiting to eat the pie until after
they'd gone.

Mr. Bonnet did buy Supaya's boxes, and gladly, for
her work was superior to others' and he could sell
them for a better price. Supaya bought several lengths
of cotton print and one of black wool to make a good
skirt. Quayo offered to make her a special dress for
her wedding, but Supaya declined her offer. Her marriage was a duty; she would dress in ordinary clothes.

At the turn of the year, Quayo and Supaya cooked
for two days, preparing for the New Year's feast, for
not one of the four hundred or so people on the reserve ate at home on that day. When all was ready,
Jules and Jacques helped carry the dishes to the Council Hall, then drove around the reserve with a wagon
picking up the elderly who were unable to walk any
distance.

The Council Hall was a large, two-story frame building with a large vestibule inside the front entrance.
There were storage cupboards, rows of hooks for wraps,
and, at one side a wide staircase to the second floor.
The inner door opened onto one great room where
tables would be set end to end in the shape of a large
U, with chairs along only the outer sides of the U,
leaving the inner space free for the serving of food.

When Quayo and Supaya arrived shortly after midday, many families were already there, and the vestibule was crowded with people hanging up coats and exchanging greetings. The women carried in dishes and placed them on the tables, now covered with white cloths. Large platters with a whole goose or a ham or venison or pork roast were placed at intervals around the table, with bowls of vegetables—potatoes, baked beans, turnips, cabbage, corn—bowls of cheese, bread, scone, and fruit pies.

All elderly people were seated and served first, being the ones most honored on this day. Quayo sat next to her cousin Em, and there was much laughter and recalling of previous feasts and the prodigious amounts of food eaten.

Upstairs, the program had already begun. The band chief spoke first, speaking from a platform that extended across the width of the room at the far end. In the slow, deep voice he thought appropriate to the occasion, he described the trip he had made to Ottawa with Mr. Jackson and one of his councillors to petition the government to restrain white fishermen from encroaching on Indian waters. Then he reminded the audience that next summer was election time and he hoped that they would reelect him as their leader for another term. His audience sat on benches and chairs and listened respectfully, the men smoking their pipes.

As the older people finished eating and went upstairs, their places at the table were taken by younger generations. Jules sat down with Cyrus Red Sky. When Supaya, who had been serving her family and relatives, went to serve him, she found Rhea ahead of her, filling his plate with the choicest food as though it were her right to do so. Resentful and embarrassed that this girl with the reputation of a flirt should pay such attention to her father, Supaya left the room and went upstairs.

A group of men singers had just finished singing a hymn and were beginning another. Reverend and Mrs.

Harris were there, sitting at one side of the room. Feeling the distaste she always felt at the sight of Reverend Harris, Supaya crossed to the other side and joined Maud and friends her own age who were waiting to hear their younger brothers and sisters perform.

When the hymn singers stepped down, Miss Harris, somewhat agitated at being the focus of attention, shepherded her students on stage. The older children lined up behind the younger, trying to disassociate themselves from the little ones, who bumped shoulders, rolled their eyes and, catching smiles in the audience, burst into giggles. Miss Harris, seated at the piano sounded the note on her pitch pipe, but they made a false start because one little girl was waving at a friend and her companions were trying to pull her hand down. At a second, sterner sounding of the note, they began again and sang the song they'd practiced for three weeks, their voices and attention fading on the verses, gathering strength and volume on the refrain.

Miss Harris then announced that Elizabeth White Cloud would recite a poem. A short, round-faced little girl with bangs stepped forward. Having been told not to hang her head, she raised her chin and gazed wide-eyed down her snub nose at the audience. With singsong precision she recited five verses expressing hope for the New Year. Then she closed her mouth with a satisfied air and stepped back into line, where friends leaned over to whisper compliments to her.

Miss Harris sounded the note for the closing selection. Now that their part was nearly over, they had come to feel at ease on stage and burst into song, finishing together on a discordant but clearly triumphant note. The audience clapped their approval, and the singers scattered, throwing themselves into the arms of their families to be petted and praised before going downstairs for more food.

After the children's performance, the Harris family

left. Supaya and Maud went looking for Kineu and
Jacques, whom they found leaning over the upper ban-
ister, exchanging banter with friends below. Most people were upstairs now, the elders seated along the
walls. Young and old settled themselves to listen attentively to Keewahd'n, an old man with iron-gray
braids, recount an experience of his youth.

He spoke with songlike cadence and great variation
of tone, his voice as soft as a whisper or so deep and
resonant it filled the room and vibrated against the
walls. He was a famous speaker, one of several old
men who took turns telling stories of their past. Raising his arm in a slow, sweeping gesture, his eyes looking into the past, he recreated for them all their former
life of freedom, with no reserves, when the people
were free to roam as they pleased and lived in harmony with their Mother Earth, enduring hardships
with courage and strength.

He spoke of the Four Hills that all men must face:
the first to be climbed in infancy, the second in youth,
the third in middle age, the fourth in old age. He described the struggling young ones, the many who failed
while climbing the first hill, who fell weak and gasping, never to rise. How sorrowful to see hope die, how
saddened their brothers and sisters who could not
pause but were driven to push on, scarcely stopping
when their companions fell beside them. On they must
go, climbing up the second hill and the third, despite
the hazards of steep cliffs, narrow, rock-strewn paths,
and paths that led nowhere. What pain they feel, looking back at their struggling loved ones! How hard to
call out encouragement but be unable to touch their
outstretched hands! The fourth hill was most frightening, the steepest of all, with the sharpest rocks. The
words of those who reached this hill were most valu-
able, for they had climbed all four hills and had at-
tained much wisdom. Those few who were fortunate
enough to reach the top of the fourth hill disappeared

into a mist. The audience listened entranced, seeing through Keewahd'n's eyes the never-ending cycle of birth, life, death, and renewal. When he finished speaking, three old men stepped forward, one of them carrying a drum. Together they sang a song thanking the Great Spirit for the gift of life, their powerful voices swelling, fading, and swelling again as they danced in a circle, lifting their feet to the beat of the drum, bending and swaying their bodies with the agility of young men. Arms raised, they gave one shout and the dance ended.

As though called into life, the audience rose and began shoving back chairs, clearing the floor. The fiddler sprang onto the stage and tuned up his fiddle. The caller came forward and gave directions for the formation of the first dance. Kineu, quick and graceful, was an especially fine dancer, and he and Supaya joined in at once, swinging round and about, weaving in and out, down the length of the room and back, following the pattern the caller sang out. The old people sat along the sides of the room and watched, tapping their feet and clapping their hands. Jacques and Maud joined in, and Hettie and Arthur, Neegonas and James, and Rhea and a young man, but Jules stood at the end of the room, smoking and talking with a group of older men.

When the fiddler and caller took their first break and the dancers sat down to catch their breaths, six men leaped on stage and acted out a skit they had made up. One took the part of the agent, who was shown as a buffoon and hilariously stupid. The audience, quick to recognize familiar characters, called out comments and clapped with enthusiasm. Bottles of rye whiskey were passed about, and when the dancing began again, the fiddler played a faster tempo and the caller chanted his pattern, moving his shoulders and swinging his arms. The dancers skipped and twirled, skirts ballooning, feet stamping and turning, their quickness and grace inspiring the caller to more and more intricate patterns.

Outside, the winter dark came early. The old people, except for a few who stayed to watch the dancing, and the children, sleepy after so much excitement and eating, were taken home. But in the hall, lamps were lit and the fiddler played on, encouraged by shouts and hand clapping from the whirling dancers, whose faces, warm from exertion and whiskey, gleamed in the lamplight. Couples dropped out, breathless, then, caught up by the music, joined in again. After midnight both the fiddler and caller went downstairs for food and drink. Some of the dancers followed: the rest stayed to watch some bawdy skits, laughing uproariously at the tipsy actors, whose mock-serious, droll expressions and drunken, uninhibited antics they found inexpressibly funny. When the fiddler and the caller, fed and rested, took the stage again, the dancing continued.

In a dim corner Rhea pressed herself against Jules. She had a half empty bottle and she held it up, offering him a drink. Angrily, he pushed the bottle away. "I am a doctor. You know I do not drink."

"Then take me home." She slid her hand inside his shirt and smiled up at him. "I want to go home now."

"Now I am going to take the old people home."

"Ah, well!" Rhea made a face. "I will wait for you here, but if you don't come back soon, someone else will be glad to take me home."

He watched her walk away, filled with disgust for her and loathing for himself for wanting her. Without calling Jacques, who was dancing with Maud, he got together the remaining old people and helped them into the wagon. By the time he returned, it was after three. He encountered Rhea in the vestibule. She had her coat on and was leaning against a man, one arm around his neck. Seeing Jules, she smiled, patted the man's shoulder, and walking unsteadily, came to slip her arm through Jules'.

Supaya and Kineu came downstairs in time to see them leave together, Rhea holding onto Jules' arm for support, her head aaginst his shoulder. Supaya, ashamed for her father, pretended not to see him.

There was no moon, but the stars were bright and very close in an immense sky that imposed its own vast silence over the snow-covered earth. Supaya and Kineu walked toward her home, the cold pressing against their faces.

"Suppy, let me come in. Just for a while. Your father's not home."

"No." She knew her father was not home. That Kineu should refer to what they had seen touched her family pride, made her inclined to be irritable. Besides, it was her father's home, and she felt it unseemly for her and Kineu to be together there. "No," she said again.

But Kineu held her close and kissed her, brushing his lips enticingly over her face.

"I guess we could go in the barn," she whispered, "for a little while." Later, from her bed in the loft, she heard Jacques come home.

No one heard Jules. He walked silently and alone in the early dawn, past darkened houses and fields where only the fence posts showed above the snow. The stars had paled in the growing light. Only the morning star still glittered above the trees. Then clear on the still air came the long, sad, haunting cry of a wolf. Jules raised his head and listened as again, from beyond the hill, the wolf sang once more, its last falling note hanging on the cold, still air.

"Maheengun!" Jules whispered. "You are there and I would speak to you!" Suddenly he felt himself to be unclean, unworthy. Going to the pump, he held his hands in the icy water, leaned over and doused his face and head. Pushing back his wet hair, he lifted his face toward the east.

"Grandfather Maheengun, hear me! You who are
fleet as thought, pure as flame! Touch me!
For I am filled with shame! Purify my spirit!
"Oh Great Father, help me! You whose vision
encircles the world! You who see all paths!
Help me! For my sight has failed! I am weak
and can no longer find my way! Touch me,
that I may see again!
"Oh Great Maheengun, lonely hunter! Singer of
the Great Spirit! Teach me to bear my loneliness! For I am alone in the morning of
the world! Speak to me!"

Face uplifted, Jules stood waiting, all his senses concentrated, straining to hear the most distant cry.

Above the hills a delicate, rosy glow began to fan
out across the pale sky. But though he waited, listening, there came no answer.

CHAPTER SEVEN

The lake ice split with a sound like the crack of a rifle. Thick slabs of ice broke apart, moving ponderously, edge grinding against edge, up-thrusting in jagged peaks, the green-gray water swirling over half-submerged floes. In an agony of rebirth, the splitting and booming of the ice reverberated across the thawing land. Streams raced toward the lake, their swift currents carrying fallen branches and undermining overhanging banks of earth and softened snow. Roads became mires of mud and slush, and the meadows of dried, matted grass oozed water.

Home food supplies were running low for all on the island. Mr. Bonnet, who liked to keep his shelves well stocked, had emptied all his barrels and boxes; the empty shelf space grew larger week by hungry week.

Quayo still had vegetables and dried fruit, for they'd had a good garden crop the summer before, but their meat and fish were almost gone. Jules and Jacques worked hard to bring home meat, plodding miles through the woods in deep, wet snow too soggy to support their snowshoes, sinking in up to their knees in pursuit of game that was difficult to find. Fear of being caught in the freezing slush when night came limited their range. Often they returned weary and numb with cold, empty-handed or with a poor catch, thin from the hard winter and good only for soup.

Supaya, who had worked busily, even at times happily, during the bleak winter, saw with growing dread glistening drops on the ends of icicles hanging from the eaves and mud appearing in dark, soggy patches through the snow along the paths to the pump and the backhouse. But around her, others were delighted to see the melting snow and buds on bush and tree swelling to the bursting point as the sun moved north and the days lengthened. They emerged from their houses, smiling, eager to greet one another, excited and happy at having weathered possible disaster.

Supaya grew increasingly silent and moody, impatient even with Kineu. She had almost finished gathering her things together: two new dresses and a skirt lay folded in her tin trunk, along with a pair of new moccasins, a large supply of quills, carefully washed to remove the oil and then sorted and wrapped, packets of medicinal herbs and seeds from the garden. Aunt Hettie had given her a comb and a small, hanging mirror. These were in her trunk, along with a fine old buckskin blouse with quill embroidery on the neck and shoulders from Auntie Em.

"My mother made this for me," Auntie Em had said, touching the quills with trembling fingers. "I wore it when I married. You have been as a daughter to me. You take it. You wear it." Supaya had embraced her, pressing her face against the wrinkled old cheek. As she was leaving, Auntie Em called her back and put into her hand a small piece of dried, ridged root. "It will protect you on your journey." And Supaya had put it in the small pouch that hung from her belt.

From the steps of the general store, Supaya could look out over the lake. Small puffy clouds sailed high and fast above the distant moving line of free water, and nearer shore the water showing between ice floes grew wider day by day. Soon the steamer would begin its round of the lake ports, pushing aside the last, thin sheets of floating ice to bring mail and supplies to people cut off from both for nearly four difficult months.

Supaya had been able to push away thought of leaving home so long as snow blanketed the island. But now the burgeoning spring gave her departure such immediacy that Supaya wished the steamer there that very moment, so she could face the disaster of parting now instead of anticipating it day after day. She felt herself already separated from her family, even from Kineu. Daily she saw them living as they would when she was gone. Their home was no longer hers. It had taken on the sadness of a dearly remembered place where once she had been happy. She lived in a vacuum, having no one and no home to take the place of those she was deprived of.

As she was on her way back from the store, Miss Harris called to her from the steps of the school building, holding the door with one hand and waving with the other to attract her attention.

"Sophia, do come in for a moment. I'm so glad to have seen you." Supaya followed her into the schoolroom, breathing the familiar odor of chalk, paste, and children's bodies.

"I've missed you these last years, Sophia. Now I hear you are moving away, going to the mainland to be married."

"Yes, Miss Harris. I have to go when the first steamer comes."

Miss Harris clasped her hands together on her desk and looked searchingly at Supaya's sober face. "That will mean a big change for you, won't it."

"Yes, ma'm," said Supaya, looking down.

Agatha stretched out a hand toward her, then drew it back. "Who is the young man you are to marry? Have I ever had him in class?"

"Oh no, Miss Harris. He has never lived on this reserve. I do not know him, but his name is Eli Red Sky."

Miss Harris stiffened. "You don't know him?"

Supaya shook her head. "No, Miss Harris." Agatha's shocked face made her feel as if she'd made an inexcusable mistake in simple arithmetic.

Agatha stood up, crossed the room and looked out the window, her back very straight. Trying to contain her disapproval and show only the sympathy she felt for this young girl of whom she was so fond, she turned and asked gently, "Is there anything I could do to help you, Sophia? Would you like me to speak to your father or grandmother? Or to my brother, Reverend Harris?"

Supaya, shocked by the alarming possibility of Reverend Harris' causing a terrible scene, exclaimed forcibly, "No, Miss Harris! It's all settled!"

Agatha was confused. "You mean you don't mind marrying a stranger?"

Supaya stood up and faced her proudly. Her words were courteous, but distinctly cool. "It is my duty. It has been well arranged."

Agatha, hearing the formal words and seeing the father in the daughter's haughty, impenetrable eyes, knew that she was to presume no further. "Well, Sophia, I am sorry you are leaving us." She turned to her desk. "I have something here I want to give you." Her tone softened. "You were my star pupil in reading, you know." She smiled shyly at this confession and held out two books. "I'd like you to have these."

Surprised, Supaya took them with both hands and smiled, too delighted to speak.

"Well," laughed Agatha, pleased by her response, "don't you want to look at them and see what they are?"

One was a leather-bound copy of the Holy Bible; the other a copy of Dickens' *Hard Times,* bound in dark green with a border of entwined flowers, and on its flyleaf Agatha had written: For Sophia, a fine student, with best wishes, Agatha Harris.

"Thank you, Miss Harris," said Supaya. Agatha's

fond expression made Supaya suddenly aware how much she owed to this woman, what a bond there was between them. The late afternoon sun streamed into the quiet, dusty schoolroom, and for the first time in weeks, Supaya was on the verge of tears. She dropped her eyes and murmured, "I will keep them always, Miss Harris, and I will remember you always."

"Just be sure you read them," admonished Miss Harris briskly, walking her to the door. "You must keep up your reading."

"I will, Miss Harris," promised Supaya.

"We won't say good-bye, Sophia. When I visit the mainland, I will be sure to come and see you." Again she put out her hand, and this time permitted herself to pat Supaya lightly on the shoulder. "I hope you will be very happy in your new home, Sophia."

One day in late April when the snow lingered only in the woods and even there only along ridges and under banks, Supaya and Kineu went out to gather wild leeks, the first green vegetable to thrust its pointed shoots through the freshened earth. Given a firm tug, the leeks came out with damp soil clinging to their pale brown bulbs and hairlike roots. Supaya found a good-sized patch and, moving along, bent over, had half filled her basket when a sudden dizziness overcame her. She sank down on her knees, her head hanging forward.

"Suppy! What's wrong?" Kineu caught her round the waist and helped her up. "Come, sit on this rock."

"Nothing's wrong, Kineu. I'm tired, that is all." She had felt tired all week and faint once or twice before. She tilted her head back for the fresh breeze to dry her damp forehead.

All around them plants were budding or coming into leaf. Morels, their crinkled skin tan or velvety dark brown, had pushed up through the layers of dead leaves. Bright yellow trout lilies, dogtooth violets, with sun-speckled leaves already bloomed along the slopes.

Branches, with buds pink and swollen, stirred against a blue sky where crows sailed and tilted in the limpid air, settled in the swaying treetops, then lifted off again in answer to a distant cawing. Supaya sighed contentedly and smiled at Kineu, kneeling beside her. "I wish we could stay here like this forever." Then, matter-of-factly, "Oh well, Grandma is waiting for these." She began sorting through the leeks, brushing off the dirt. "There are a lot this year. We'll soon have enough."

Kineu took a package from his basket and held it out in a childlike gesture. "Suppy, this is for you." What he felt but was unable to express was: When you put this shawl around you, it will be my arms around you, warming you with my love. Instead, he said, "I wanted to be sure to give it to you before . . ." He stopped, then forced himself to finish, ". . . before you go."

Surprised, Supaya unwrapped the package and held up a dark blue woolen shawl. "Kineu! It is beautiful! I'll put it on now!" She shook it out and drew it about her shoulders. "There!" She looked up, expecting his admiration, but saw only pain in his eyes and knew that he was not seeing her but himself without her. "Oh, Kineu!" In a burst of anguish, she took his head between her hands. "Don't look like that! Please don't!" But the pain in his eyes remained, and she cradled his head against her breast, stroking his hair, murmuring his name, rocking slightly back and forth as if comforting a child. Leaning against her knees, he embraced her fiercely. His muffled voice shook with unshed tears.

"You are leaving me! You promised me! Yet you are going away to marry him! I should go and kill him! I want to kill him!"

"Kineu! Don't say that! You know why I must go, why I *must* marry him! There's nowhere we could go where we'd be safe! Not my family, nor yours, nor our . . . our children!"

"You'll forget me! You'll live with him and forget me!"

"Kineu! I will never forget you! Never! I couldn't't!"

"But you're mine! Mine!" he insisted, holding her tight, his face still hidden.

"Yes, Kineu, yes." She leaned her cheek against the top of his head, forgetting her own sorrow and fear in her need to comfort him. "I will always be yours, always!"

Quayo stewed the leeks, and their pungent odor filled the house. She served them with fish Jacques had caught that afternoon. The men had just finished eating and were lighting their everyday, hawthorne wood pipes when Cyrus Red Sky came by to tell Jules that Wenonga had arrived on the steamer and would come for Supaya in the morning.

Shaken by the prospect of immediate departure, Supaya slept fitfully and rose early. She dressed in a full-skirted, long-sleeved cotton print dress with a high buttoned bodice, and the white woman's shoes she wore when she went to church. She was packing her few other clothes in the trunk when Quayo came up to the loft.

"Granddaughter, I want to give you this." She held out to Supaya a black velvet drawstring bag. "This was my father's, Negik, your great-grandfather. He was a wise man and a great healer. This was his medicine bag. He gave it to me. Now I give it to you. It has great power. I have put in it medicines for illness and medicines against evil. Look, I will show you." Quayo took out the medicine packets and laid them on Supaya's bed. "All these I have already taught you. But this one, *nimepin,* is to be used against witches, and this one against envious wishes and those who would harm you. Look, it glows. When you have it near, you will know you are not alone. You will be protected. Take great care of these. Use them wisely. You will be a stranger and may need to protect yourself."

Then she took out a pair of moccasins beautifully decorated with glass beads. Brilliant red, yellow, blue, and white beads had been painstakingly sewed on the skin in a fanned-out, sunlike design, a blaze of color against the pale buckskin; the sides were bordered with a geometric design in deep greens and white. "These I made for you. May the path you walk in them be safe and happy."

"Grandma, they are the most beautiful you have ever made!"

"It is a design I used once for your mother, when she married your father. Now you may use it." Last, she took out a case made of birchbark bound with sweet grass and tied with leather thongs. "I made you this housewife. You will need your own now."

Supaya untied the thongs. Inside was a flannelette lining holding needles of various sizes, threads, and a special bone awl for her quill embroidery. This was a particularly fine one, smoothed and shaped, Supaya knew, by many hours of patient work, difficult for her grandmother's weak eyes and stiff fingers. She held it in her hand and looked at Quayo, her eyes glistening with tears. "Oh, Grandma," she whispered, hiding her face against Quayo's shoulder, overwhelmed with a sense of loss in parting from this old woman who had been both mother and teacher.

Quayo embraced her and smoothed her hair. "Ah, Granddaughter, do not mourn. Part of me goes with you, and you will live in my thoughts always." Hearing Supaya cry, she said, "Do not be afraid. You will be a good wife. We will be proud of you. And remember, you have a great blessing in your Grandfather. You can always call on him for help."

Supaya sat up and drew a long, quavering breath. "Yes, Grandma, I will remember." She managed a smile and said, "I will come back and bother you often."

Downstairs a door opened, and the women heard voices.

"Come," said Quayo. "Wenonga is here." But before they went down, Supaya took off her blue stone necklace, for the first time since her father had placed it around her neck, and left it behind, lying on her bed.

Wenonga had come, wrapped in his blanket as before, but carrying gifts not only of tobacco, but of flour, sugar, and tea as well, all very welcome after a long winter. He was disposed to be friendly, his bulging, fiery eyes now more curious than suspicious. He sat at ease and smoked his wooden pipe with Jules and Jacques, whose polite, distant manner hid the pain they felt at Supaya's departure.

Supaya greeted Wenonga briefly and went calmly to the wash bench in the lean-to where she began carefully combing and braiding her hair, clearly taking what time she pleased.

Quayo served the men tea and scone, which they ate in dignified silence. Wenonga observed Supaya's preparations, and when she finally put on her coat, drew Kineu's shawl over her head, and picked up her carpetbag, he rose to go.

Then Jules addressed Wenonga in a stern, deliberate way that commanded everyone's attention. His voice was edged with a threat that none of them failed to hear.

"Wenonga, I have paid my debt. I have given you my daughter, Supaya, who is dear to us. We have cared for her, protected her. Now it is you who must act in our place. She is going among strangers, and it is you who must see that she is safe and well cared for so that when we next meet, we will rejoice in our daughter's well-being."

"My son and I will care for her," answered Wenonga. "Our home will be hers."

Jules turned away and stood by the fireplace, his

back to them all. When he heard the door close behind them, he looked sharply at Quayo, who sat with her hands folded in her lap.

"Quayo, she was not wearing her necklace!"

"No," said Quayo. "I saw her take it off. For the first time since you gave it to her. She left it behind." Quayo saw his pain, then his fear, and said quickly, "Do not fear for her. She is protected. Her guardian is with her still." Jules bowed his head and said nothing. Quayo rose and laid her hand gently on his arm. "Your child is not lost to you. She is too young to know forgiveness. Keep her necklace for her, and one day she will want it back. You will see."

The steamer was late. Supaya, and Jacques, who had accompanied her and carried her trunk, waited by the wharf. A bright sun glittered on the choppy water that slapped against the pilings and the stony shore, wearing away the remaining rim of ice. The sun was warm, but the wind blowing off the water chilled their faces. Supaya held her shawl close under her chin and narrowed her eyes against the wind.

They heard the steamer's whistle blow as it rounded a point of land, signaling its arrival. It rode high in the water, having unloaded its freight on the outward trip. Returning, it would pick up mailbags and a few passengers. Wenonga preceded Supaya up the gangplank and entered the enclosed passenger section, expecting she would follow. But Supaya went instead to the stern and sat down on a narrow bench attached to the ship's side. Jacques put her tin trunk beside her, then left the steamer and stood on the pier.

Water frothed and boiled as the steamer, with one blast of its whistle, backed up and got underway. It veered out at an angle and to Supaya it seemed that the whole shoreline swung around and the general store and wharf rapidly receded. Jacques, a lone, diminishing figure, stood with his hand raised in farewell until he was lost to view as the entire scene shifted. Auntie Em's house appeared, surrounded by trees, and standing on a rock at the water's edge was another figure. Though she couldn't see his face, Supaya knew it was Kineu. He gave no signal, but Supaya, huddled on the bench, her back to the cold wind, kept her eyes on him until he and the shore sank into the lake and only the trees stood above the water.

Then it was that she saw, above and beyond the woods, the hill where she had dreamed. She had never before seen Stone Island from such a distance, and never had it looked more beautiful. In the bright morning sun it seemed to float on the sparkling water. Rising out of the deep green of pines and firs, the hill stood out sharply against the clear blue sky. Gazing at it, Supaya was transported. She felt herself sitting once again in the little hollow, the boulders protectively above her, sunlight glancing off their sides, with only the boundless expanse of heaven above her. . . .

A shaft of light, glinting on the water, struck her in the eyes. She blinked, recalled from memory, and saw that Stone Island had sunk below the horizon. Only the vast lake stretched behind her, its choppy water foaming in the steamer's wake, curling outward in a constantly repeated pattern. Supaya leaned against the rail, her bag close beside her, her trunk at her feet. She faced backward, conscious only of the ship's pulsing, forward rhythm.

PART TWO
1901-1907

CHAPTER EIGHT

All day Wenonga watched Supaya through windows that in warm weather opened onto the back deck. Wrapped in his blanket, he sat as immovable as she, ignoring the other passengers, who glanced at him, then sat apart, conversing among themselves. He saw her raise her head when the steamer docked at stops along the way and knew she watched for his appearance on deck as a signal they had arrived. He saw one of the deckhands speak to her and when she lowered her head and pulled her shawl across her face, ignore her. He expected she would be driven inside by the bitter wind, but now, as the late afternoon sun slanted across the deck, he knew she would not. The steamer had rounded the lake and was headed northwest. They were almost at their destination.

Wenonga envied Jules his strong daughter. He envied his son, Eli, having her for a wife. She had dreamed. Unusual for a woman. And that dream had given her great power, which he respected. He wondered about the extent of her power. How long could she match herself against him? She would be too strong for Eli. Concentrating, he willed her to raise her head and look at him, but she remained still, her face hidden. It was good she had such strength, as well as beauty, for Eli would be too weak for her, and then he, Wenonga, would subdue and possess her. Watching Supaya, he thought how it would be to take her young, seductive body, and for a while his weak son, a sorrow for Wenonga, ceased to exist.

Indifferent to any scrutiny, Supaya withdrew into herself, enduring the chill, numbing wind and giving no thought to the food Quayo had packed for the journey. She simply sat, unfeeling, almost unseeing, while water and time flowed past. Whenever the steamer docked, she looked for Wenonga. Not seeing him, she scarcely noticed when they again put out from shore.

As the ship veered northward, the declining sun touched her cold face and shone in her eyes. Squinting ahead, she saw great reddish stone bluffs rising straight out of the lake, their tops green with trees to the very edges. Then the steamer swung about, throwing out a great curving backwash. The land opened out, revealing a long, narrow bay and a city whose buildings rose in tiers from the shore to the tops of the surrounding hills. Wellston, Ontario, was a small, grimy town, its largely frame buildings thrown up during a lumber boom, since declined. But it was such a town as Supaya had never seen or imagined. The steamer's steady pulse slowed to a heavy throb as it entered the narrow bay where gulls, dipping and soaring, filled the sky. Supaya was amazed to see not one but many piers lined with fishing boats; not one store and a house or two, but many buildings, two, even three stories high, leaning together, their steep, gabled roofs forming a jagged, irregular line. Only the width of a cobbled street, lined with buggies and wagons, separated the buildings from the seawall.

The steamer whistled and sidled in alongside a wharf where men ran forward with ropes. Passengers emerged from the cabin and clustered together, waiting for the gangplank to be lowered, Wenonga among them. Awed and fearful of being separated from him in this strange place, Supaya clutched her bag, braced the tin trunk on one hip, and came quickly to stand behind him.

The gangplank down, Wenonga strode ahead, moving with proud, stately dignity among dockhands and stacks of freight. Cunningly, he did not look back, leaving Supaya to follow as best she could. Supaya tried desperately to stay close behind him, but her trunk, heavy and awkward, impeded her. She veered sideways to avoid bumping one man only to bump into another, who turned and spoke sharply to her. For a moment she lost sight of Wenonga and in her panic tripped on the rough planking, almost losing her grip on the trunk. She grabbed for a better hold, and an old man with a bristly gray chin and a stocking cap pulled down over his ears laughed at her. He was warming his hands over a fire in a tin drum.

"Fair loaded down, ain't ye?" he remarked, grinning at her through the tatters of smoke that blew up from the drum.

Supaya instantly averted her eyes and hurried on, dragging the trunk and hearing the old man's rasping chuckle behind her. Looking ahead for Wenonga, she saw that he had reached the street.

A dog, standing guard in a wagon, saw Wenonga and began barking. Infuriated, the animal leaped down and rushed forward, snarling, his lips curled back over his teeth. Front legs stiff and splayed in mixed anger and fear, he lunged at Wenonga, forward, then back, yapping hysterically, his eyes rolling wildly. Supaya shrank back, horrified. People turned and stared. But Wenonga, impervious to all that did not concern him, ignored the frantic dog and turned his head slowly, looking for his son.

Two men came from around the wagon. One reached out for the dog's collar.

"Hey, get back here! Back in the wagon!" He jerked the frenzied dog almost off his feet and swung him around. Half choked, the dog persisted in a half-strangled barking. "He never could stand them Indians, but he don't usually carry on so," the man said to his companion. He gave Wenonga a suspicious look and slapped the dog, who leaped, quivering, back up into the wagon.

Unconcerned with both man and dog, Wenonga saw Eli and started toward him. Following his glance, Supaya saw a young man coming directly toward them. He appeared tall and very slim in a dark suit and black felt hat that shaded his face. Overcome at his approach, Supaya lowered her head.

Eli had left the wagon at the end of the street. He had been there, sober and waiting, when the steamer arrived, and had watched with amusement his father's and Supaya's progress toward the street. Wenonga had told him Supaya's name and the many benefits he would gain by having as wife the daughter of a respected healer and one well-trained in the old ways. Eli had not objected. He liked women. This marriage pleased his father and his Aunt Nonen. He had nothing else to do; he might as well take a wife.

Eli met them just as a piercing blast of sound split the air. Supaya, nerves already tight, gasped and jerked up her head. Starting with fear, her eyes met Eli's. He was struck first by the loveliness of her face, then by her fear. He had seen blind panic in animals, had experienced it himself. He put out his hand sympathetically.

"Don't be afraid. It's only the train whistle." He saw she didn't see him, didn't understand what he'd said. "Here, I'll take your trunk. The wagon is at the end of the street, Father."

Wenonga strode ahead. Supaya followed automatically, eyes down, scarcely breathing, hardly daring to look up. Walking beside her, Eli could see the tenseness of her hand as she clutched her shawl to her chest.

The wagon was small, pulled by a brown, shaggy horse who stood patiently, head drooping, one foot cocked. Eli lifted the trunk and carpetbag into the back and would have helped Supaya up, but she stepped quickly onto the wheel hub and over the side. Seeking at least a partial refuge in which to regain her composure, she huddled down on the wagon bed behind the driver's seat, her head bowed against her drawn-up knees, all but hidden by her shawl and long skirts. Her head was spinning. For a few moments, she was dimly conscious of the sounds of the street, people talking, drivers yelling and cracking whips, wagons jolting over cobbles, and above it all the raucous cries of the gulls. She heard Wenonga speaking to Eli, then felt the wagon swerve as it moved out into the street. As they rode along, the street sounds faded until she heard only the clop of the horse's hooves on the cobbles. She raised her head as they turned up a steep, graveled street with stone or brick houses on either side. Supaya looked with wonder at these houses, several stories high with long, narrow windows. She had never imagined a house would have so many windows or doors decorated with glass fans. Abruptly the gravel ended, and the wagon rolled along more quietly on a dirt road where the houses were of board and batten, small and drab and further apart.

As they rounded a curve at the top of a hill, Supaya had a sudden, brief view of the town, its streets in shadow, its chimneys and church spires still bright in the setting sun, with the lake beyond like a piece of rippled blue silk. Then the road veered north, into the countryside. They passed farms with larger barns than Supaya had ever seen and meadows where huge boulders shouldered up through the earth. Between groves of trees where darkness had already come, she glimpsed narrow bays cutting into the land, the distant water shining like silver far below the steep, rocky bluffs.

They traveled in silence except for the soft muffled sounds of the horse's steady jog, the chink and slap of harness, the creak of the wagon. Eli held the reins, and Wenonga sat beside him, his heavy head forward on his chest, Supaya, stiff and aching from the long, cold boat ride, felt every jarring stone and rut in what seemed an endless ride. With the coming of night, the air grew colder, but the sky remained clear and the evening star, a pale glimmer in the western sky, was familiar, though at home she would have seen it hanging far out across the lake. She thought of Quayo, her father, and Jacques, and of Kineu, but her sense of displacement was so great that they lacked reality. She felt she had parted from them a very long time ago.

It was quite dark when Eli pulled the horse to a stop in front of a store by the roadside. The storefront was in darkness, but inside oil lamps lit up shelves and counters and shone through the center door and two wide windows onto the long, shadowy porch.

Wenonga muttered a question, but Eli jumped down without answering and entered the store, banging the door open and shut, his figure dark against the light. Wenonga and Supaya waited in silence. The horse, eager to get home, blew softly through her nostrils.

Eli made a quick exchange across the counter and returned. He slapped the reins and they went on. Occasionally Supaya saw lighted windows and the dim shapes of houses set near the road; now and then a dog barked, noting their passing. Wenonga said something to Eli, whose answer displeased Wenonga, and he said in a louder, angry voice, "Now! It will be done now!" A few minutes later Eli stopped the wagon again, this time in front of a house. Wenonga turned. "You get down now," he said to Supaya.

Light from a single window slanted across a section of porch and a railing that split the light into bars as it fell into the darkness of a small, fenced-in yard. The fence palings were ghostly white. The gate, when Eli pushed it open, made only the faintest sound. Behind them, the tired horse, impatient for its stall and feed, stomped and whinnied, a sound apparently heard inside, for Wenonga had only raised his fist to knock when the door opened, giving the impression that he was about to strike the tall, thin man who appeared. Silhouetted against the light that shone into the hall from the side room, the man motioned them inside, saying, "Come in, come in. We were expecting you."

They followed him into the parlor, where a large oil lamp cast their lumpish shadows onto the flowered wallpaper. Light gleamed on the glossy black surface of a horsehair sofa and the polished backs of chairs. Lace curtains hung at the windows, and between the windows hung family portraits, in dark, ornate frames. On the floor beyond the edge of the rug, a row of dirt-filled flowerpots was lined up in front of the windows.

Supaya, standing back and to one side from Wenonga and Eli, was startled by the tall man's reaching out and grasping her hand with his bony fingers. "I am Reverend Crowell, my dear," he said, stretching his head forward on a neck too thin for its collar. "Welcome to Two Bluffs Reserve." His long thin face with eyes set close to a high-bridged nose expressed a solemn concern. "We have been expecting you, yes, we have, my wife and I. Mr. Red Sky told us you were coming. My wife will want to welcome you also." He raised his voice as if to summon her out of thin air.

"Mrs. Crowell! Mrs. Crowell! She's working in the back room with her plants, you know," he said to Supaya. Then to himself, "She does expend such energy! Well," bringing his attention back to his guests, "sit down, please sit down."

"We want the marriage now," said Wenonga aggressively. Eli, who had removed his hat and was about to sit down, straightened up again.

"Of course you do, of course. As soon as my wife . . . ." Reverend Crowell was about to call again when Mrs. Crowell entered. "Here you are! My dear, Mr. Red Sky has brought Eli and his bride-to-be from Stone Island. I knew you would want to welcome her."

Mrs. Crowell, who had stopped short just inside the room and looked to her husband for direction, came forward at once. "Oh yes, my dear, I *do* welcome you." A small, frail, fair-haired woman, she took Supaya's hand in both of hers and looked up at her anxiously. "You have come a long way, haven't you? I'm sure you must be tired."

Before Supaya, dazed and very tired, could form an answer, Reverend Crowell said quickly, "I think, my dear, the sooner we have the ceremony, the sooner they will reach home. The church is lit, so if you will get your coat, we'll just step next door to the vestry."

With Reverend Crowell leading the way, they walked through the gate, across to the church and down a path beside it to the rear entrance, passing in and out of the light shining from the high, narrow windows. In the vestry, a small room with a few chairs and a desk where each week Reverend Crowell struggled over the composition of his Sunday sermon, they all removed their coats except for Wenonga, who stood aloof in his blanket.

"Why don't you let me take your shawl, dear," said Mrs. Crowell. Without waiting for an answer, she drew it off and folded it over her arm. Then, touching Supaya's elbow, she guided her into the church and indicated where she and Eli should stand.

Supaya, who had not yet brought herself to look directly at Eli, was conscious of his shoulder and arm beside hers. She focused her eyes on the book in the preacher's hands and heard him intoning as Reverend Harris used to do, but was too fatigued to pay attention. She repeated automatically when asked twice or prompted gently by Mrs. Crowell. And when Eil stood ready with the ring, Mrs. Crowell had to whisper, "Hold out your hand, dear," which she did, like an obedient child, and saw, as though it were happening to someone else, Eli put a gold band on her finger.

Back in the vestry, Reverend Crowell filled out the

certificate. He bent over the desk, the lamplight shining through the sparse brown hair that lay across his pinkish bony scalp, and wrote, murmuring the words to his pen.

"Now, if you will sign here, please." Eli and Supaya wrote their names where Reverend Crowell's finger pointed, then Mrs. Crowell, as witness, and Wenonga, who stepped forward, grasped the pen boldly and made his mark. Reverend Crowell held the paper up, pursed his lips, and blew on it.

"You must keep that," he said, handing it to Supaya, "and show it to Mr. Toomis, the agent, tomorrow."

Without looking at it, Supaya folded it away into her pouch. Wenonga turned immediately to the door. Mrs. Crowell had been watching Supaya as she might a plant with drooping leaves. Stretching up her arms, she draped the shawl around Supaya's head and shoulders, holding the ends together for a moment as she looked intently into her eyes.

"I hope you'll be very happy, my dear. Once you are settled, you must come and visit me. We'll have a cup of tea and I will show you my plants."

Through her weariness, Supaya saw the kindness in Mrs. Crowell's pale blue eyes. "Thank you," she said, wondering irrationally about all those dirt-filled pots. Later, the one clear image she had of her marriage was Amy Crowell's face, looking earnestly up at her.

The ride to Wenonga's house was short, and the horse, knowing the way, tossed its head and picked up speed. It swung briskly into a lane and would have taken them all to the barn had Eli not pulled up short beside a house where a dim light showed through one small window.

The door opened and a woman stood on the threshold, almost filling the doorway. "*Ahnee, ahnee,*" she said, her voice deep and resonant. Eli, holding the trunk, stood to one side to allow Supaya to enter.

"Come in, come in. Welcome to your new home. Eli, put her trunk in the bedroom." She turned to Supaya, who had stopped just inside the door. "I am Eli's *noshan,* his aunt." Like her brother, Nonen had a strong, broad stature, wide face, wide mouth. She was older than Wenonga. Her braided hair was gray, and her face had many fine lines. But she had a commanding, energetic presence and a sharp eye. She saw Supaya's sagging shoulders and heavy eyes.

"You have had a long journey. Take off your coat and sit down. We will have some tea."

Supaya hung her coat and shawl on a peg, then carried her bag to the table and took out two packages of dried berries, several strings of dried apples, some maple sugar, and a small jug of maple syrup. "My grandmother, Quayo, sent you these," she said. Speaking aloud the loved name and handling the familiar objects made her separation from her family all at once very real, the distance she had come very great. Her lip suddenly trembled, and she put her hand to her head.

Nonen set the teapot back on the stove and came instantly to put an arm about Supaya's shoulders. She drew her to her own rocking chair beside the stove.

"There, sit and rest." She spoke kindly to Supaya, who closed her eyes and rested her head against the chair back, but her eyes flashed angrily at Wenonga, sitting stolidly on the other side of the stove, and at Eli, just coming in from stabling the horse. "You have not taken good care of her! She is worn out." Her quick eye saw the gold band on Supaya's finger. "You should have brought her home first! Time enough for that tomorrow!"

Wenonga glanced at Eli, then back at his sister, but said nothing. Nor did Eli, who was looking at Supaya.

Nonen made a disgusted sound and reached for the teapot. She poured them each a cup of tea and took out of the oven a pan of warm bannock which she put on the table. Supaya started to rise, but Nonen said, "No, sit there," and brought the bread and tea to her.

The bread tasted unbelievably good to Supaya, who had not thought of eating all day, and as she finished one piece, Nonen brought her another and poured her more tea. As she ate, eyes downcast, she was conscious that the others, seated at the table, were talking, Nonen having asked Wenonga about their relatives on Stone Island. Their conversation became a quiet, almost comforting murmur. The initial shock of arrival was over, and warmed by the hot tea, Supaya gradually relaxed. Heat radiating from the large stove warmed her cheeks and caused her wind-burned eyes to droop uncontrollably, though she strove to keep them open. Her arms and legs grew heavy, then ceased to have any feeling at all. The room, the voices faded. Unable to rouse herself, she drifted into sleep. Her eyes closed and her head slowly tilted sideways against the chair.

At the table, conversation ceased. They all came and stood looking down at her. Gently, Nonen took the tea cup from Supaya's limp hand.

"Get her up," said Wenonga, reaching out to shake her.

"No!" said Nonen sharply, extending her arm protectively in front of Supaya. "Leave her alone! Go to bed and let her sleep!"

Wenonga's mouth drew down contemptuously. But after a moment he turned without a word, went into his bedroom, and pulled the curtain across the doorway.

Eli gazed thoughtfully at this sixteen-year-old girl who was now his wife. He had no wish to wake her. He understood the shock of displacement. Tomorrow she would feel better and they could talk.

Beside him, Nonen regarded Supaya with all the sympathy of her commanding nature. Thoughts of herself as a bride, and of her daughter, combined to focus all her maternal, protective impulses on this young girl asleep in her chair. She had finally acquired, in her old age, a second daughter. "You are lucky, Eli," she said softly. "She is very pretty."

"Yes," agreed Eli, "I am," realizing that for the first time in his life he had something of his own. She is mine, he found himself thinking in surprise, mine!

CHAPTER NINE

After a week of rain and blustery winds, the weather suddenly turned fine. Together Nonen and Supaya planted the garden. Working parallel rows, they sowed the seeds leisurely, enjoying the spring warmth, pausing to chat or notice who was passing by. But Supaya was really watching for Eli, who had gone in the wagon for supplies. As she worked the earth, her long hair fell forward, and she stopped to twist it around and tuck it out of the way, smiling to herself remembering how that morning Eli had caught her by her hair as she was getting out of bed and had pulled her back into his arms. He had laughed at her faint protest, drawing her hair to one side over her bare shoulder and breast, telling her she would never get away from him for he could always catch her by her hair. Now it seemed to Supaya he had been gone far too long, and she listened for the wagon.

Eager to return to Supaya, Eli came at a faster pace than usual. Nellie, enlivened by the spring air, needed little urging. Eli pulled her up near the lean-to, and she tossed her head as if to free herself of the reins, her rounded flanks gleaming red-brown in the bright sun. Jumping down, Eli carried the sacks inside, then came jauntily toward the women.

Supaya thought him very handsome. His hair parted naturally on one side, a strand habitually falling across his forehead. His eyes were large, like his father's, but clear, and his nose, broken in a childhood fight, had a slight bend, an irregularity that increased rather than lessened his attractiveness. He had the broad shoulders and developed muscular arms of a man of twenty-six. He crossed the rows they had planted, careless where he put his foot and grinning at their cries of protest. He halted in front of Supaya and threw out his arms.

"Who cares about planting on such a day! Come, let's walk to the bluff."

"But we're not finished! We have other rows to do."

"Do them tomorrow!"

Supaya looked at Nonen, who said, "Go. Go. I will finish." Nonen was happy to indulge them, happy to see Eli gay and smiling, instead of sitting about the house sullen and morose.

"Come! You have to do as I say," said Eli, laughing and throwing down Supaya's spade. He caught her hand and pulled her along past the barn, across the rocky meadow where Nellie usually grazed, and into the woods. Half-opened leaves were lacy against the blue sky, and sunlight, shining through, dappled the tender green undergrowth.

They walked close together, bodies touching. Eli found it hard not to touch his lovely, obedient young wife, and when they smiled at each other, the memory of their lovemaking was in their eyes. He was grateful, now, to Wenonga, for Supaya had given a focus to his empty pointless existence. As never before, his heart swelled with a vague, undefined hope for the future. With her, he felt sure his life would take shape.

Supaya was at home in these woods, which were very like the woods on Stone Island, more at home than in Wenonga's house. Although his was larger than her father's, had a bigger stove and two bedrooms downstairs instead of one, and a loft as well, she was not at ease in it. She missed the open fireplace, and Wenonga's presence pervaded the house. She felt his burning watchful eyes on them even in their own room with the curtain drawn across the door. She did not feel sufficiently comfortable to hang up her mirror and still kept her things in her trunk. But out in the garden or the woods, with Eli or Nonen, she was content.

The woods ended at the edge of the bluff. Though Eli had brought her there before, Supaya was always surprised by how high above the lake they were. A narrow bay cut deeply into the land and at its inner end the bluff sloped down to a rocky shore, but where they stood, facing outward, the water rippled far below sheer layers of striated, reddish rock.

Where a rocky outcropping formed a partial cave, they sat down and looked out over the sunlit water where gulls lazily rose and fell in the clear air, their white wings flashing as they floated in long, banking curves down between the bluffs.

"The land at home is rocky too," said Supaya, "but we have no bluffs like these," nodding toward the opposite side of the bay. "The woods are the same. And we would be planting now too."

"Stop talking about what you did there! This is your home."

Supaya turned toward him. "Don't you want to hear about my home? My family?"

Eli met her eyes briefly; then his glance slid away, down over her rounded belly. "No. I don't. This is your home now," he insisted. "You forget all that. *I* am your family."

"But, Eli, I can't forget . . . ."

"Yes, you can. I'll make you!" He pulled her close, and holding her chin firmly, brushed his lips tantalizingly back and forth across hers as he whispered, "I will make you forget them all!"

And for a time she did forget, for Eli was a practiced lover. Supaya, knowing only Kineu's youthful outbursts of passion, reached eagerly for Eli's teasing kisses, responding spontaneously and ardently to his lovemaking. Eli, used to a calculated coyness, was enthralled by her innocently passionate response. For the first time he felt deep satisfaction and pride in his own masculinity and a new, exhilarating sense of power. He liked bringing her to the bluff, for here he'd discovered she was freer than in their room at home.

Afterwards, they lay stretched out, luxuriating in the sun. Supaya's head was on his chest, her mind at peace. The sun warmed her legs, bare below her rumpled skirts, and glowed red-orange through her eyelids. She raised one arm to shield her eyes. Then it was that she heard, or sensed, something or someone watching. In one swift movement she rose to her knees and looked sharply around at the tumbled boulders, the still trees. Only the tilting, mewing gulls circled endlessly above the bay. But her ears caught a faint, retreating sound.

"What is it?" asked Eli, squinting up at her.

"I don't know. Eli, let's go. There's work to do."

Eli rolled over and put his head in her lap. "Work! Who wants to work!"

Supaya smiled down at him. "I do," she said, stroking back his hair. "I want to help Nonen with the garden."

"You're supposed to help me, and I need a kiss."

Supaya laughed. "One," and bent down.

"More," he commanded, embracing her.

But Supaya, remembering the unseen presence, was uneasy and pulled away.

"Go then!" said Eli, pretending indifference. "You don't even know the way back."

Amused at such an idea, Supaya laughed and held out her hand. "Come. I'll show you the way."

Eli, pleased to humor her, got up and took her hand. But he led the way.

After the first day or two, Supaya had easily adjusted to her new home, even finding excitement and challenge in her new position as wife. Nonen treated her as her own daughter, welcomed her help, praised her work, and made easier whatever she could. Only Wenonga made her uneasy, his eyes constantly on her. But often he was gone all day. When he was home, Nonen and Eli were there too.

Eli had been adroit. At ease with her himself, he had put her at ease. The first day, after she was rested, he showed her the garden and the barn and made her laugh by introducing her formally to Nellie, whose flank shivered under her hand. They spent all day together, and he was amusing and companionable. There was little resemblance between him and his father, and for that Supaya was glad. She even thought him handsome. His broken nose was prominent, his chin angular, and his mouth, slightly unsymmetrical, gave his face a whimsical charm. And his admiration of her was apparent.

That night, when they were alone, he gave her a present, the one he had stopped at the store to buy for her on the way home, a hair comb of tortoiseshell set with cut steel in a lacy pattern. He approached her slowly, with soft eyes and a gentle hand. He caressed her long hair and told her she was to twist it up and wear the comb after the fashion of white women. In bed he stroked her as he stroked Nellie until, aroused and all constraint gone, she had embraced him with an unexpected ardor that flattered him and increased his desire for her. In the days following, they were constantly together, and though he made no public display of his affection, his eyes would linger on hers, possessive and enticing. Supaya, with no thought of the future and no questions for a present so full of love and warmth, rapidly settled down. The bitterness and sadness she had felt all winter were gone, replaced by a happiness she had never expected.

Her pregnancy, soon recognized, was accepted without comment. Nonen, delighted at the prospect of a child in the house, cautioned her about her diet. She mustn't eat the flesh of porcupine or the baby would be headstrong, with a prickly nature; or suckers, lest the baby have too large a head. Until the birth, Nonen flatly refused to serve potatoes, for they were white man's food and a contamination. She constantly asked Wenonga to bring home whitefish, trout, and venison. He grumbled but would return with the desired catch, flinging it down before Nonen as if answering a challenge, once bringing of his own accord a deer's head to ensure the baby's having good thick lashes and brows.

As her belly grew larger, Supaya looked forward eagerly to her child's birth, smiling to herself when she felt it move. At such moments she thought of Kineu and was filled with wonder, puzzled by her own happiness. She touched the shawl Kineu had given her, so long ago it seemed, reemmbering how much it had meant to her, how she had worn it proudly, as a kind of shield. And she was filled with pained confusion when she remembered holding him against her, comforting him with promises. She loved him still, she knew, but Eli was her husband, and he had made her love him also. Happening to look up, she encountered Eli's soft, dark eyes watching her, a slight, sensuous smile curving his lips, and she folded the blue shawl carefully and sadly, and laid it away in the tin trunk.

One day Nonen thought it time to take Supaya to the store with her. Eli, having risen late as usual, was drinking his breakfast tea. Supaya, wearing Quayo's old shawl, stood before him.

"Eli, can I have some money, please? I need paper and pencils. I want to write home."

"Home?"

Abashed, Supaya said, "To my father and grandmother and brother, to tell them I am all right."

"I have no money," said Eli shortly, drinking his tea.

"I will buy them with the supplies," said Nonen,

intervening. "Come, we'll go now." Eli said nothing more and did not look up as they left.

The silence between the two women was strained. Since the day she had come, Supaya had not known Eli to go hunting or fishing either by himself or with Wenonga. Nor had he gone to work on the reserve or at a lumbering camp. Except for occasional trips for supplies, he was always with her. The money Nonen spent was Wenonga's. Supaya glanced sideways at Nonen.

"Doesn't Eli work? Has he no money of his own?"

For the first time Nonen was evasive. "Sometimes he repairs harnesses. Sometimes he helps build a barn or house." She paused, then added, "He looked for work in Wellston, but there were no jobs for him." Seeing Supaya's expressionless face, she did not add that he often stayed several days in Wellston, returning in a surly, mean temper, his clothes dirty and ill-smelling. Or that when he did earn a little, he spent it on drink.

"Does he never hunt or fish?"

Nonen, hesitating to tell Supaya the truth, finally did so. "He is not a good hunter or fisherman. He was sent to government boarding school. He never learned how to hunt and fish. They taught him to read and write, to mend harness and nail boards together." She appealed to Supaya for understanding. "They took him when he was very little, when his mother died. They even beat him for speaking his own language. Now he has no skill."

Supaya knew Eli had been at boarding school, but had not realized she was marrried to a man who could not bring home meat or fish and who had no craft. How could he provide for their own home, which Supaya hoped to have, or for children? Wenonga was a good provider, as good as her father and Jacques. Why did Eli not go with him and learn so that they would not always be dependent on Wenonga? These questions were like a weight on her mind. She said nothing further to Nonen, but she was determined to speak to Eli as soon as they were alone.

Down the road they passed the school, a building very like the one Supaya had attended, and beyond, the church where she had been married. In the front yard of the parsonage, Mrs. Crowell was down on her knees, taking weak, spindly plants from pots and putting them into the ground. Seeing the women, she sat back on her heels and said good morning, inviting them to stop; but Nonen, upset by their conversation about Eli, gave her a brief good morning and went on. All the eagerness drained out of Amy Crowell's face, though she tried to smile. Supaya, sorry to see her disappointment, promised to come another day, very soon, feeling sympathy for this little woman who seemed as unsuited to her location as her plants.

The general store was just outside the reserve boundary and was larger than Supaya had thought. Like Mr. Bonnet's, it was a gathering place for both Indians and whites. Men lounged along the edge of the porch, their hats tilted forward, shading their eyes. Others sat with their backs against the building, hands hanging limp over their drawn-up knees. As the women approached, conversation ceased and heads turned, following them as they came up the steps and crossed the porch.

Supaya, unused to such staring and ill at ease with her hair swept up, was grateful for Nonen's presence and passed them all with her chin lifted and eyes straight ahead. Inside, a white woman with blonde hair was helping three young Indian women. As Nonen and Supaya passed them, the girls turned, nudging each other and whispering. Nonen stopped at the side for grocery supplies. Supaya went past the yard goods and wearing apparel to the back of the store, where there were general farm and household supplies. She was scanning the shelves when a man spoke close beside her.

"Well, you're a long way from home, aren't you?"

Startled, Supaya turned. A tall white man with curly black hair smiled down at her. He wore no hat this time, or coat over his fancy vest and white shirt, but she remembered instantly his intense blue eyes laughing at her over a pot of soup. He was amused at her surprise, and his amusement deepened with pleasure when he saw she remembered. Out of her embarrassment, she said, "Yes," then, flustered, "No. I mean, I live here now."

"You transferred to this reserve?"

"I got married," said Supaya primly, looking away.

"Ah," he said and made a little bow. "Welcome to Two Bluffs, Mrs. . . . ?"

"Red Sky," said Supaya, disconcerted by his bowing. At his slightly startled look she added, "Eli, Eli Red Sky."

"Oh yes," he said, his eyes flicking over the comb in her hair. "Well, Mrs. Red Sky, what can I help you with?"

"You know Mr. Fallon?" asked Nonen on their way home.

"I saw him once," answered Supaya. "He came to Stone Island, to our store." She said no more, pretending not to notice Nonen's curiosity, but she felt herself blushing unaccountably.

"That store is his," said Nonen, and added, without looking at Supaya, "That white woamn with the yellow hair is his wife."

So he married too, thought Supaya, and immediately wondered at herself. Why shouldn't he marry. Anyway, what did it matter?

That evening she wrote a letter home. Eli sat across from her, watching suspiciously every word she wrote.

"What did you say?" he asked.

"Just that I am well and . . ." but before she could finish, he reached across and, to her astonishment, took the letter and read it.

"Who are these men you send greetings to—Jules, Jacques, James, Kineu?"

Supaya took a moment to control her anger, then answered, each word flat and distinct. "They are my relatives, the ones you didn't want to hear about. Jules is my father. Jacques is my brother. Neegonas, whom you left out, is my sister. James is my sister's husband, Hettie is . . ."

Eli, hearing her anger, glanced up and, surprised to see her narrowed eyes and thin lips, said placatingly, "All right, all right!"

But she would not stop. ". . . my aunt, Kineu is my cousin, Maud is my friend and future sister-in-law. Why," she asked coldly, "don't you read it aloud? Then Nonen and Wenonga could hear it also? After all, they paid for it."

Embarrassed and intimidated before his father, Eli shrugged and tossed the letter back.

Wenonga, smoking his pipe by the stove, watched and listened, his reddened eyes alert and calculating, like a hunter sighting the first tracks of his prey.

Nonen stood up. "It is late. We should go to bed."

Supaya folded the letter and put it in an envelope, announcing as she did so that she was going to read for a while. Getting the Dickens book Miss Harris had given her, she opened it on the table and began to read silently.

Nonen went up to the loft, and Wenonga, the ghost of a smile on his lips, walked soundlessly to his room and pulled the curtain.

Eli sat still, waiting for Supaya to look at him, but she did not. She was too angry to give her full attention to reading, but after an interval she turned a page and continued. Eli rose, and going around the table, put his hands on her shoulders and rubbed the back of her neck with his thumbs. At his touch, Supaya's anger began to fade, but still she didn't move. Eli bent over, rubbed his cheek against hers.

"Come on, Suppy," he murmured, and reaching out turned the lamp very low. When she didn't protest, he turned it off altogether and slipping one arm around her waist, drew her up into his arms. At first she stood stiffly in his embrace, but as he kissed her, hard and long as if to draw out all her anger, her defenses melted, and he thought she repented of her fit of anger. But later, lying close against him, listening to his even breathing, she thought drowsily that he had not said he was sorry, and as she fell asleep, she resolved not to write another letter in his presence.

The next day Eli made a show of going with Wenonga to help repair a neighbor's barn. Eager to mail her letter, Supaya walked alone to the store. On the way back, she stopped at Mrs. Crowell's house, but not seeing her about, took a smaller, back road as a shortcut home. As she walked along, she heard voices behind her. She paid little attention until she realized they were speaking about her.

"Look at her! That's what they raise on Stone Island!"

"Girls so dumb they marry because they're told to! How can Eli stand her!"

Supaya glanced around and saw they were the same three girls who had been in the store the day before. She walked a bit faster, thinking they would fall behind and she would not have to listen. But they walked faster also and came even closer.

"She had to get married, that's why! Poor Eli didn't know he was getting a family!"

"Somebody ought to tell her he already has a family!"

"She thinks she can get away with it! But I'll show her! She can't steal my man!"

Shocked by their words, Supaya walked on as though

she hadn't heard. Angered by her show of indifference and determined to provoke a reaction, they came closer still.

"Go on, Marie! Make her sorry! Show her no back-woods girl can come here and take our men!"

"Beat her up! That'll show her! Make her go back where she came from!"

There was a sudden hush as Marie, skipping forward, stuck out her foot and, catching Supaya's ankle from behind, tripped her. Supaya pitched forward, sprawling on the dirt road. Before she could roll over, Marie threw herself furiously on Supaya's back, landing with a force that took Supaya's breath and caused a sharp stab of pain in her belly. Marie snatched out Supaya's comb and threw it aside, where one girl stomped on it, smashing it to pieces. Marie fastened her hands in Supaya's hair and yanked back with all her strength. Supaya grunted with pain, drew her arms back under her, and thrust up and sideways, throwing Marie to one side.

"Hit her! Hit her!" shouted one.

Supaya and Marie rolled over and over, hitting with their fists, gouging, twisting, and kicking, their hair loose and flying, dust rising in a cloud about them while the other two circled round, urging Marie on. Striving to hurt Supaya's face, Marie raked her nails down her cheeks. Supaya, with more deadly intent, grabbed Marie by the throat and pressed both thumbs against her windpipe. Marie arched back, her mouth gasping for air.

"Grab her hands! Grab her hands! She'll kill her!" The two girls caught Supaya's arms and pulled back hard, breaking her hold on Marie's throat. As they twisted her arms painfully backward, Marie, wild with rage, pressed one arm across Supaya's face and began ripping away her clothes. Torn with pain, Supaya opened her mouth wide against Marie's arm and bit down hard on the soft under flesh. Marie screamed and threw herself off Supaya. Frightened by that, the others dropped Supaya's arms and backed off. Supaya drew her arms close against herself and sat panting for breath, her hair hanging about her face, the sickening taste of blood in her mouth.

Marie stared aghast at her bleeding arm. "She bit me! She bit me!"

"Kick her!" yelled one girl. "Kick her."

Needing no urging, Marie kicked Supaya viciously in the belly. "I'll show you!" she hissed. "You go back where you came from or I'll kill you!" She kicked again, hitting Supaya full in the side. Supaya doubled over in a convulsion of pain, vainly trying to protect her belly. "You hear? I'll kill you!" Marie kicked, again and again, short, powerful kicks. The others moved in and kicked her side, her back. "Go home! No one wants you here!"

"What are you doing!!"

Startled, the girls turned. Unnoticed, a young woman had come up behind them, her expression one of horror and anger.

"Marie! Betty! You should all be ashamed of yourselves! Get away from her!" As they didn't move, she threatened them. "Go on! Get away! Just wait until your families hear what you have done!"

Sullenly, the girls backed off. "She's a man stealer! She deserves to be kicked!"

"And look!" Marie thrust out her arm, red and swelling. "Look! She bit me!"

"You've done something much worse! You should *all* be beaten for what you've done! Now get along off!"

"Come on, Marie!"

Marie followed, then turned, taunting Supaya. "Just you remember! I'll get him back!"

The woman leaned over Supaya, who sat hunched forward, her arms across her belly. "Can you get up if I help you?"

Supaya raised her head. Her hair, covered with dirt, hung across her smeared, bloody face. Her eyes glittered with anger and pain.

"I'm Susannah King. I live just over there. Let me help you home."

But Supaya suddenly turned away, crawled to the side of the road and retched, her whole body convulsed. When she finally stopped, she stayed on her hands and knees, head hanging, unable to move any further.

Susannah put her arms gently around her waist and lifted. "Come on," she said softly. "I'll help you home."

For a moment Supaya hung limp, then, bracing herself, she got shakily to her feet. Susannah kept one arm around her, and Supaya leaned heavily against her. "Red Sky," she said faintly.

"That's not far," said Susannah. "Let's try."

They moved slowly down the road, stopping at intervals when Supaya clutched Susannah's arm and doubled over in a spasm of pain. When they came within sight of the house, Nonen, working in the garden, caught sight of them and came running. She wasted no time on questions. Between them, the two women half carried Supaya into the house and eased her down in Nonen's rocker. Supaya, breathing in shallow panting breaths, rested her head back, her eyes half closed, her hands hanging limp. Susannah was telling Nonen what had happened when Wenonga and Eli returned.

"See!" burst out Nonen, rushing at Eli, "see what that trash of yours has done to her! Your father told you what she was!"

Stunned, Eli backed away, staring at Supaya but saying nothing.

Wenonga came to Supaya at once and studied her closely, his flaming eyes intent and professional. He laid his wide heavy hand gently on her forehead, examined the cuts and bruises on her face, then put his fingertips lightly on her belly, feeling for life within. After a moment's silent concentration, he growled deep in his throat and turned on Eli. "You have caused this!"

"Me! That's crazy! I had nothing to do with it!"

"Do not lie! That girl shames her family! Now she has harmed us, and it is you who have brought this harm upon us!"

Thoroughly frightened, Eli shrank before his father. "Everything is my fault! You brought her here, not me! It was you, this time! You!"

Enraged, Wenonga started toward Eli, but Nonen spoke up sharply. "Stop! You'll make everything worse. We must help her!"

Susannah, embarrassed at hearing private matters, spoke softly to Nonen, "I will go now. I'll come back later to see how she is," and left quietly by the back door.

Eli, unable to withstand his father's furious stare, turned and left the house.

Nonen washed Supaya and combed her hair. Wenonga bathed her cuts with an infusion made from the roots of the wild rose, elm, and bitter-root, then applied a plaster made from the crushed leaves of the boneset. Mixing the infusion with spring water, he gave it to her to drink.

Supaya's throat was parched, and she drank gratefully. But soon a restlessness seized her. Gritting her teeth with the effort, she managed to stand up. Nonen reached out to steady her, but Supaya motioned her away. Despite the persistent pain in her side, she began walking back and forth, pausing, breathless, to grip the edge of the table or a chair back when spasms doubled her over. Nonen and Wenonga, quiet and watchful as cats, let her pace.

Though Supaya, preoccupied with the stress of her body, seemed oblivious to her surroundings, her inner

perception was painfully sharpened. In the glaring light
of humiliation, she saw herself for the stranger she
was in this house and among the people of this reserve. Nonen and Wenonga, the very furniture and
walls of the house, all had a life of their own together.
For her, an alien, they meant confinement, not secu-
rity. She saw her husband helpless, her marriage, like
a cracked bowl, coming apart in her hands. She saw
she was all but alone. Going into the bedroom, she
pulled the curtain, shutting out the sight of their faces.
She took out the stone bear and cupped it in both
hands. Leaning her head against it, she addressed her
guardian in an almost silent whisper.

> "Grandfather! Help me! I am lost among strang-
> ers! My soul is in anguish! Help me, who
> am weak and without hope!
> "Great Spirit! You whose courage is undying!
> Strengthen my heart or I am lost forever!
> "Great Bear! Your spirit is in all things, even
> one so weak as I! Help me be worthy of my
> forefathers!"

By nightfall Supaya knew her child would be born
soon—too soon. Unable to rest, she still paced. Eli
had not returned. Wenonga smoked his pipe and kept
a watchful eye on Supaya while Nonen made preparations.

She spread a clean quilt on the floor of Supaya's
room and placed on it two chairs, four hands apart,
and laid a log across the seats.

The birth was slow and difficult. Kneeling between
the chairs, Supaya grasped the log and pushed, breathing in short gasps. Her battered, discolored sides pained
agonizingly with her straining. Beside her, Nonen, an
experienced midwife, wiped her forehead and moistened her lips but would not let her drink. She spoke
tersely, encouragingly, telling her when to bear down

and when to relax. Finally, her chest braced against the log, Supaya made one tremendous effort, and the baby came. Nonen received it and laid it aside.

"Push!" she commanded, "once more."

Supaya gasped with pain as Nonen pressed down hard on her abdomen.

"There," said Nonen softly, "now you are finished."

Exhausted and dizzy from effort, Supaya clung to the log, resting her wet forehead against it. There was no cry of the newborn, and she knew before Nonen spoke.

"It is a son, stillborn."

At her words, Supaya began to whimper, then to wail, long, drawn-out, anguished cries. Wenonga, who had been excluded during the birth, came at once.

"Let her mourn," he said to Nonen, who was vainly trying to soothe her, "let her mourn!"

At that moment Eli banged open the front door. Hearing Supaya's cries, he staggered to the bedroom and leaned against the door frame, grinning drunkenly. "Cryin', eh? I have jus' what she needs! What we all need!" He held up a nearly empty bottle and lurched forward. "This'll do it!" He almost fell over Supaya, kneeling on the quilt, her forehead to the floor. Wenonga grasped him and dragged him back. Nonen, furious, twisted the bottle from his hand.

"What evil have you brought into this house! You bring shame upon us all with your ignorance! You have no right to enter where there is birth! You will be polluted by this blood! You will harm her and yourself! Never," she spat at him, still held by his father's powerful hand, "never bring this," shaking the bottle at him, "into this house again! You hear me? Never!" Turning to the window, she emptied the remaining liquor outside.

Suddenly enraged, Eli wrenched himself free and slapped Nonen across the face, knocking her back against the wall. "Who do you think you are, old woman! Don't give me orders! Neither of you! Jus' a couple dumb Indians!" Wenonga reached for him, but Eli swung around, stumbled over Supaya, and grabbing one of the chairs, raised it up and slammed it into the wall. "An' you!" sneering at Supaya, "whyncha get up! Get up and go knock old Marie down! You make fuss over nothin'! Nothin'!" He tilted unsteadily toward her, his eyes glazed. "That's what I am! Nothin'! But if I'm nothin', what are you?" Peering at Supaya, he nearly fell, but Wenonga hauled him back onto his feet. Eli, pulling to get free, yelled at Supaya. "You aren't too good t'marry me and have 'nother man's kid, are you! Not you!" Struggling with Wenonga, he lost his footing and crashed down on the splintered chair. Awkwardly he got onto his knees, oblivious to a bleeding gash in his arm from the split wood. Dazed and weaving, he pointed at Supaya. "I know what you want! You're no diff'rent! You're . . . le' go! Lemme go!" Wenonga, twisting his arm behind him, forced him to his feet, propelled him out of the bedroom and out of the house.

"Go sleep in the barn!" growled Wenonga, thrusting him away with such disgust and anger that Eli stumbled forward, arms flung out, and fell face down on the ground. Wenonga looked down at him. "That's where you belong!"

When Wenonga returned to the bedroom, Supaya was sitting on the bed and Nonen was wrapping the dead infant in a blanket.

"Give him to me," said Wenonga, holding out both hands. The infant's face was tiny and wrinkled, the thin skin over its closed eyes delicately veined, its mouth slightly puckered. "So," said Wenonga, his voice deadly quiet, "Marie Able did this. She will be sorry." He handed the baby back to Nonen. Looking at Supaya, distraught and exhausted, Wenonga remembered the charge her father had laid on him. "Do not fear," he said. "She will never attack you again." Then he turned and went to his own room.

Nonen brought Supaya hot tea and scone. "Eat this, then sleep," she urged. "I will be back soon."

There was a spring in the woods where Nonen and others went for water of special purity. And it was to the path leading to this spring that Nonen went, carrying a shovel and the dead infant and afterbirth wrapped up securely together. The sky was just beginning to lighten, and she moved swiftly, like a gray shadow. She did not wish to be seen, for the preacher would be displeased and demand a Christian burial. At the point where several paths merged into one and many women passed, she dug a grave and laid the bundle in it. Then she knelt and whispered.

"Great Father! Hear me! See this pure and helpless soul! Forced into life too soon!
"Great Spirit! Giver of all life! Give this soul life again! Help it to be reborn!"

Then she filled in the grave and tamped down the earth, treading over it and switching the dirt with a branch to hide all traces.

When she reached home, the lamp still burned, but Supaya had fallen asleep sideways, her battered face sad in repose. Nonen saw with satisfaction that the cup and plate were empty. Gently she lifted Supaya's legs up onto the bed, covered her with a blanket, and turned off the lamp. Then she pulled her rocking chair squarely into the bedroom doorway so no one could enter. Tomorrow she would clean the room. She settled into the chair and rested her head back with a sigh. Her face ached where Eli had hit her, but far worse, her arms felt empty. She had hoped to rock a baby to sleep. She pulled her shawl close, down over her face. Now she must rest so she could care for Supaya, and then, perhaps . . . .

CHAPTER TEN

Marie's arm hurt; it was swollen and inflamed. But she got no sympathy from Eli. When she unwrapped it and showed it to him, expecting he would comfort her, he shrugged and offered her a drink. Resentfully, she rebandaged it and refused the drink, knowing it angered him when she refused.

"You didn't make her drink when you brought her here!"

Eli focused his bloodshot eyes on her. "So you spied on us!" His lip curled in contempt. "Sneak!" He had not been home in a week, not since Wenonga had thrown him out. Nor had he been sober. He had bottles hidden in the barn and one in the rockfall on the bluff. He sat slumped against the stone, glowering at Marie, seeing in her round, petulant face a threat to his happiness with Supaya.

Putting aside her resentment, Marie knelt beside him. "Eli," she said earnestly, "what do you want with her! You don't have to stay here! We could go away, together! We could take Jimmy with us. We could go to Wellston and you could get a job." She laid her hand on his arm. "Please!" she begged, "let's go now!"

"A job!" he said bitterly. He threw off her hand. "Don't talk stupid. Nobody will give me a job! Think I haven't tried?" His voice rose angrily and he waved the bottle at her. "What can I do? Tell me! You and your plans! Tell me what I'm fit to do!" He leaned toward her threateningly, raising his hand sideways as if to strike her. As she drew back, he said spitefully, "You, now. You have something you can sell. Why don't you go sell it and get off this stinking reserve!" Her eyes filled with tears, and he turned away, disgusted. "Ah, go 'way. If you're not going to drink, go 'way."

Knowing further talk was useless, she got to her feet. But as she was leaving he looked after her and said with a malicious smile. "You better be careful. My father knows it was you beat her up, and he's angry."

Walking back through the woods, Marie held her throbbing arm against her plump waist and thought about the rashness of her act—attacking the daughter-in-law of the shaman! What a fool she'd been! She should never have let Betty goad her into it! Wanting Eli back so bad, wanting to hurt his wife and drive her away, she had not thought until Eli's words reminded her that she'd brought on herself the wrath of Wenonga. The realization of what she had done, the danger she was in, wiped out all other worries. Eli wouldn't help. Nor could her own family. No one could help her. Though the day was warm, a tremor ran through her and a hard knot of fear felt like a weight just under her breastbone.

Hearing a sound behind her, she turned, hoping it was Eli, but there was no one, only the shine of sunlight on leaves. Alarmed, she walked on, faster. Again she heard something, a soft rustle in the underbrush. Nervously she turned, hoping to see someone, anyone, but again there was no one, only the sun-dappled leaves, unnaturally still. There had been a breeze. Now the woods were deadly still, hostile. She felt eyes were watching her. She went on, walking fast, almost running, certain that she heard a light, panting breath behind her. Panicked, she broke into a headlong run, snagging her clothes, stumbling over roots, running into branches that scratched her face and arms. Heart pounding, she suddenly emerged onto a road. She saw a man and a woman with a bundle, strangers, walking along. They walked straight on, not speaking or turning their heads. Not daring to look back or to pass them, she forced herself to a walk that kept her behind them until she reached the house where she lived with her father and stepmother. She would not go into the woods again. Not alone.

That night as she was falling asleep, she heard a dog barking in the distance. The barking came closer and grew louder, a deep-throated, powerful bark. As it came nearer, she listened with growing fear, her nerves tight. All at once the barking ceased. She waited, but all was quiet. She finally relaxed and was closing her eyes when suddenly, just outside her window, there was a long, low growl. Instantly, she was wide awake. Crouching on her bed, she slowly raised her head, peered over the windowsill, and screamed in terror. There, as if waiting for her to appear, was a huge dog. His white fur glowed in the dark, luminous as the moon; his hackles rose thick and bristling along his back and neck. His eyes gleamed red with rage, and as she stared, hypnotized, his black lip curled back and he lunged at her, snarling, his sharp teeth snapping together. Marie tried to scream, but no sound came. Shaking with fear, expecting him to crash through the window, she dropped down and cowered under the bedclothes. There was another vicious snarl and a long growl. Then the barking began again, circling round and round the house. After what seemed a long time, the barking receded and finally faded away.

The next day, pale and shaken, Marie went outside and searched the ground. But there had been no recent rain, and the earth near the house was hard and dry.

Her father and stepmother were disturbed. They looked at her uneasily and wouldn't speak until she left the room. Then she heard them whispering. They knew, as everyone on the reserve now did, of her attack on Wenonga's daughter-in-law.

Later that day, Jimmy ran into the house, frightened and crying for his mother. A big dog had come after him, growling and snapping at him, a big white dog, and he held up his hand even with the top of his head. Aghast, Marie clutched him close and looked pleadingly at her father. His eyes like stones, he stared back at her, then left the room without a word.

That night there was a storm. Great jagged streaks of light split the black clouds, lighting the earth in lurid flashes. Thunder crashed and reverberated over the bluffs. Rain blew in gusts, drumming like hail against the windows, drowning out all other sounds. When the lightning receded to incandescent gleams far out over the lake and the thunder to a soft, distant rumble, the barking began again.

Angrier and more aggressive than before, the dog stalked round and round the house, a persistent, deadly hunter. He stopped by Marie's window, his bark deepening to a throaty snarl and then a long, implacable growl. Marie lay rigid in her bed, scarcely breathing, listening to scratching and snuffling alongside the house. Only thin boards separated her from those powerful jaws. Suddenly there was a jarring impact as the dog flung himself against the house. Paralyzed with horror, Marie felt the wall shudder and heard sounds of splitting wood as the huge animal attacked again and again. Then he moved off, still barking, as before, until his voice faded away.

A pall lay over the house. Her father and stepmother were speechless, their eyes bright with fear. Jimmy clung to her, refusing to let go his hold on her skirt. Outside they found impressed in the damp earth huge paw prints, larger than any they had ever seen. The wall outside Marie's room was damaged, the boards splintered where they had begun to split and bend inward.

Her father drew his wife aside, and they conferred privately. But Marie did not wait to be asked to leave. She packed a bag and asked her father to take her and Jimmy to Wellston in the wagon.

They rode in strained, chilly silence despite the bright sunlight that cast along the roadside a skimming shadow of horse and wagon. When they passed through areas where the woods grew close to the road, Marie watched fearfully. Once, smothering an impulse to cry out, she thought she glimpsed the sun gleaming on a white form slipping through the underbrush. She didn't see it again, but just before they turned out of the reserve onto the main road, they heard behind them, startling in its nearness, a deep, strong, aggressive barking.

The horse laid back its ears. Her father struck out with his whip. Marie held Jimmy tight and pressed her fist against her mouth as they moved faster down the road and the barking gradually faded.

CHAPTER ELEVEN

In old moccasins and a light cotton dress, Supaya walked along a gravel road on her way to meet Susannah. She and Soos were going out to pick sweet grass to dry for trimming boxes and making mats. The day was good for it. There'd been no rain for a week and the fields on either side shimmered under a hot, hazy July sun. Preoccupied with her thoughts, she didn't turn when she heard a wagon coming but kept to the side of the road. As the horse clopped past, trailing a cloud of dust behind it, a voice said, "Whoa, boy," and then, "Good morning, Mrs. Red Sky. Can I give you a lift?"

Supaya glanced up, her eyes flat. "I am going only a short way."

"A short lift, then," insisted Jess Fallon, smiling. He reached out to give her a hand up, but she ignored it. Rather than argue, she stepped up lightly and settled herself with her basket on her lap, her eyes straight ahead.

He snapped the reins and the horse stepped out. They rode in silence, he stealing glances at her as they went along. She had been in for supplies several times that summer when the cuts and bruises were still livid on her face, and he had felt concern for her. He had seen her pass the loafers outside disdainfully and turn with cold indifference from the curious eyes of women in the store. He couldn't know that she had accepted her position as a stranger in the community in addition to being the daughter-in-law of a feared shaman, and that now she imposed her own distance between herself and others. But he did observe that no one presumed to comment or question her. He saw that now her face was healed—Wenonga was a skilled doctor. And she was much thinner—too thin, he thought—though he admired the sharp, clean line of her cheek and jaw. But he missed her liveliness. Her spirit seemed to have fled, leaving only a shadow of her former self.

"Here," she said suddenly, with a nod of her head. She got down, said a brief thank you, and walked away.

Jess looked after her, noticing she wore no comb but had coiled her hair into a knot low on her neck. And despite her apparent lack of animation, her step was vigorous, her carriage as proud as when he had first seen her on Stone Island. Given a little more time, he thought, she would be all right. He shook the reins, feeling unaccountably happier.

When Supaya and Susannah had filled their baskets with sweet grass, they sat down near the stream to rest. Supaya lay back, her whole view the tops of wild meadow grasses and a vast blue sky with scattered puffs of clouds. The air was filled with the pungent, spicy aroma of weed and wildflower. Grasshoppers chirred and leaped, and a cloud of gnats hovered, moving mysteriously together in the radiant heat. The earth was solid and warm under her, and Supaya sighed, smiling faintly.

"It's nice here, Soos. Here I feel at home." When she had first set out to look for sweet grass and had found this meadow, she had been struck by its similarity to the one in her dream, and she had seemed to hear again the soft laughter of her mother. She felt at peace here, warmed alike by sun and memories.

Susannah would not presume to advise, but she and Supaya had become, during the past few weeks, good enough friends for her to ask, "Couldn't you have your own home, Suppy, you and Eli?"

"There is no empty house," said Supaya. In her rambles around the reserve, she had seen several abandoned houses, but their windows and doors were gone, their roofs caved in, and weeds grew up through the floors.

"Sarah," called Susannah, shading her eyes to look after her small daughter. "Come back."

Sarah came, her plump knees pushing through the grass, holding up a fistful of wild daisies. Delighted to find Supaya lying down, she plumped across her middle and offered her bouquet. "For you!"

"Sarah," chided Soos, "get off!"

"No, no," said Supaya, "I'm not sore any longer." She was fond of Sarah, and catching her under her arms, bounced and twisted her from side to side while the child giggled and went limp, amused at being flopped about.

"You could ask Mr. Toomis. He might know of one."

Supaya had met Mr. Toomis her first day on the reserve, when she had taken him her paper of transfer and shown him her marriage certificate. A younger man than Jackson, and much pleasanter, he had invited her to sit down while he recorded names and dates.

"If you wish, I'll go with you to speak to him," promised Soos.

For the first few days after the stillbirth, Nonen had insisted Supaya rest, and had brought her food, tempting her with fruit and soft, white cheese. For a week she had guarded the room every night should Eli return. She tried to comfort Supaya, whispering that she had buried her son where he might yet have a chance for life, if not with her, with someone else.

But Supaya, aching for the life she had felt within her, for the child that would have been hers and Kineu's, cried at night, eyes staring into the dark, while hot tears wet her cheeks and ran down into her hair.

During the day when Nonen allowed her to get up, she sat in Nonen's rocking chair and thought of what she could do to make money. Most of all, she wanted her own house, to be independent and free of Wenonga's constant presence. For that, she needed some money. She could not depend on Eli, who had not returned, and could not bear being dependent on Wenonga. She had her quills from home, but she had no birchbark.

One day Nonen offered to get her a supply of bark. Shortly after Nonen left, Wenonga came home. He was surprised to find Supaya alone, and leaned over her ostensibly to examine the healing of her face. He brought his face so close to hers that she felt his breath warm on her cheek. His red-veined eyes gazed compellingly not at the healing skin, which he touched gently with his fingers, but into her eyes. Supaya stared back defiantly, her head pressed against the chair back, then, as he persisted, his face almost touching hers, she turned her head sharply away.

"Your cuts are healing," he said softly, and laid his hand on her belly, moving it caressingly back and forth.

Repelled and frightened, Supaya pushed his hand aside and sprang to her feet. "But your son," she exclaimed, "has not returned! Where is my husband? Surely, it is your duty to find him." Wenonga frowned. Seeing him hesitate, she said scathingly, "My father would think it strange I should come this far to marry a man who disappeared! If he is gone, I should return to my family!"

Wenonga, balked, knew she spoke the truth. "He is here . . . in the woods, the barn. You have not been well."

"Now is when I need him most," said Supaya sharply. "I do not believe he is in the barn. I think he is gone and I must return home."

Wenonga glared, but she stood firm, masking her fear with anger.

"I will get him," growled Wenonga and strode out of the house.

Supaya went at once to her room, opened her trunk, and from her great-grandfather's medicine bag took out a very small birchbark box. She removed the lid and sniffed at the powdered roots, bark, and fungus inside, smelling faintly of wild leeks. "You will be among strangers," Quayo had said, "and might need to protect yourself." Satisfied, Supaya covered it and put it inside the trunk where she could reach it easily at night.

Nonen returned with strips of bark and a promise of more. Supaya was busy cutting them into pieces when Wenonga returned. Behind him came Eli, stepping as carefully as though the floor were moving beneath his feet. He glanced quickly at Nonen, who was ladling stew into bowls. The bruise from his blow was gone, but the memory of it was in her eyes as she watched him slump into a chair. He propped his elbows on the table and rested his head in his hands.

No one spoke. They began eating the stew, and after a bit, Eli, who still had not faced Supaya, began to eat also. Observing him from across the table, Supaya saw he had difficulty keeping his spoon steady. His face was gray, his shoulders sagged. She could not forget his violence toward herself and Nonen, but he was her husband, and seeing him thus stirred her sympathy. Somehow they must make a life together; somehow she must help him.

"You need a bath," she said.

The unexpectedness of her remark made Nonen laugh. Even Wenonga was wryly amused. Eli, who thought to hear only recriminations, looked up in bleary-eyed surprise.

Nonen began at once heating water for the tub. She

was grateful for Supaya's matter-of-fact acceptance of Eli's return, for it seemed to her an assurance that after a bad time their lives would happily resume. Wenonga, smoking his pipe and watching Supaya making boxes, did not think so.

That night, Supaya took out the little medicine box, removed the lid, and placed the box on top of the trunk on her side of the bed.

Eli, still puzzled by her apparent unconcern over his behavior, asked what she had.

"It is a protection," she answered coolly, undoing her hair, "against anyone who would harm me. Get in bed. I will turn out the lamp." In bed he moved to embrace her, but she pushed him firmly away. "I am not ready," she said. "You need rest. Tomorrow we must talk." And she turned on her side so she could see in the dark the glow given off by Quayo's medicine.

At her invitation the next morning to come for a walk, Eli's assurance began to return. He thought she meant to go to the bluff, that she was ready to forget what had happened. But Supaya went only as far as the meadow, where they could speak without being overheard, and sat down, facing the house and barn so she could see if anyone approached.

"Eli," she said, "we should have a house of our own."

"A house of . . . ! Why?" he asked, mystified. "We don't need a house. We are fine where we are."

"We *do* need a house! We should not live off your father."

Eli stared. "How . . . I can't get a house! I have no money!" Immediately restless, he stood up, wanting to go.

"You have no job," corrected Supaya quietly. "You get a job. Then we will have money. Then we can get a house."

Desperately, Eli looked about at the rocks and grass as if searching for an answer. Seeing her waiting for a reply, he drew a deep breath, trying to control his nervousness, then spoke slowly and distinctly. "I cannot get a job. There is no steady work for me on the reserve. And in town the whites will not give me a job."

"But you went to school! You can read and write!"

He turned on her angrily. "They don't pay for knowing how to read and write! Hear what I say! I have tried!" He had said all this before, to himself, to his father and Nonen, to Marie, and now to her, his wife, whom he could not support. He knew he had been cheated, robbed of identity. He was at home nowhere, and years of humiliation and fruitless grappling with the problem had drained him of stamina. Mulling it over was painful. He wanted only to turn his face away, to forget. "I need a drink," he said and started for the barn.

"No! Please, Eli! Wait! If you can't get a job, then we will hunt and fish. We could use Wenonga's boat and I will help you! We could make our own garden, and I can sell boxes. We could make enough that way, I know we could!"

Exasperated, he stared at her. "I'm no fisherman! Or hunter. Don't you understand! I'm nothing! Ask my father if you don't believe me. He is a great hunter. He even brought me home a wife I can't support—and a child!"

Out of his shame, he wanted to hurt her, but she was angered. Before his taunt had been that of a drunken man. Now he was sober. She regarded him with hostility. "*My* son," she said coldly, "is dead. *Yours* is alive."

Eli showed his teeth in a sharp grin. "Come on, we both need a drink."

"No."

"Come on, I said! What kind of wife are you? You do what I say!"

Giving him a scornful look, Supaya started for the house. She had tried and failed. If he would not help, she would work alone. As she passed him, Eli grabbed her arm. She spun around, eyes blazing with anger. "Go find Marie! She'll drink with you!"

"Marie?" Eli grinned again. "She's gone! Wenonga saw to that. He protects his own. You should be careful!"

That she must be careful of Wenonga Supaya already knew. Why couldn't Eli see that she needed him as he needed her! "Eli," she said urgently, "please do not drink! You pollute yourself! You waste what skill you have and become no better than the white man. I will not drink with you ever. And I will not be as a wife to you drunk."

But Eli only shrugged, and she left him standing in the meadow.

The need to make a living now occupied all Supaya's waking thoughts. Her days were filled with gardening, preserving food, making boxes, and weaving table mats of dried, pungent sweet grass to sell at the general store. When she lay down at night, her grief, buried during the day, came out unbidden, stealing over her heart, and with it worry over Eli and Wenonga.

Since their talk in the meadow, Eli had been sleeping in the barn, and one night, as Supaya undressed, she felt a prickling across her back. Turning swiftly she saw Wenonga's shaggy head at the window. His face was shadowed, but his eyes, reflecting the dim lamplight, gleamed as he stared in at her. Instantly she turned out the lamp, then stood trembling, ears straining for the faintest sound. She heard the front door softly open and close. She waited as if frozen, eyes fixed on the dark, curtained doorway. But the curtain didn't stir. After a long time, Supaya got silently into bed, lying so she could see the pale greenish glow from the birch box.

Early the next morning a man came for Wenonga. His child was ill. He begged that Wenonga cure him. At once Wenonga began preparations, ordering Nonen to make him a sweat lodge.

When Eli came in from the barn, Supaya was waiting for him. After her fright of the night before, she resolved to try once more. "Eli, today we can use your father's boat. We can go fishing, you and I."

His head ached, but he was sober. The morning air had a fine freshness and Supaya, her eyes pleading, took his hand. Grudgingly, Eli agreed. He knew locations where his father fished, but, he warned her, "I don't know the currents. We could get caught in a storm." The day was clear and dry; a storm seemed unlikely.

"Besides," said Supaya happily, "we won't go too far out."

Wenonga's boat was a good one, and Supaya, who had not been fishing in a year, was happy to be out on the lake again. She pretended not to notice Eli's awkwardness with the oars. That he had come at all she saw as encouraging. He would learn, she was certain. They paralleled the coast, rowing northward past a part of the reserve Supaya had never seen. When they reached a narrow bay, Supaya took over the oars and Eli let out the net.

By midday they moored the boat and walked along the narrow, rocky beach, a light lake breeze offsetting the strong sun on their backs. Being away from the house and working successfully together had driven off the anger and tension of past weeks and made them feel gay, almost shy of one another. They smiled at each other sideways as they had used to do, then laughed and clasped hands. They searched for a spot to sit down and eat the food Supaya had packed. Halfway up the cliff was an inviting grassy ledge. They climbed up the pebbly incline, holding onto bushes and exposed roots. Clowning, exaggerating their breathlessness, they flopped down on hands and knees and then onto their backs, side by side. They turned their heads and gazed at each other, their eyes bright, questioning. Seeing her face soften, her lips part, Eli pulled her close against him.

"This," he said, smiling, "is the kind of fishing I like." Supaya, wanting him and seeing him as he had been when they were first married, caressed him, kissed him hungrily, her body, craving the touch of his hands, giving itself completely, mindlessly, in its desire to once more come alive.

When the sun lowered behind the bluff, casting the beach below into shadow but still sparkling on the water offshore, they came down the slope. They were less giddy but happier: each content in himself and with the other. Supaya saw her lover returned, gentle and affectionate. He would learn to be a good fisherman and a skillful hunter. Together they would make their own home. And Eli saw the Supaya of months before but relieved of her burden and freer in her passion; a young wife who, having been upset, had a fit of temper and now was once again tractable and docile.

Supaya took the oars as Eli hauled in the net and extracted the fish, clumsily at first but with increasing skill despite his fumbling buffoonery. Their catch was a good one, and after putting some trout and whitefish aside to be split and dried, Eli sold the rest and came home with money in his pocket.

The next day Wenonga was performing his cure. Again they used his boat and brought home a sizable catch. This time Eli clowned less, but there was a satisfied gleam in his eye as he surveyed the drying rack hung with fish.

That evening Supaya settled down to do some quill embroidery. Laying the quills out in separate piles

according to length and color, she began the pains-
taking work, using the fine awl Quayo had made for
her.

Eli paced restlessly about the room, jingling the
coins in his pocket. He stopped by the table, picked
up one of the finished boxes, turned it about indif-
ferently, and dropped it. "There's a party at Joe Mar-
tin's tonight," he said. "Why don't you stop that and
come."

Supaya carefully inserted a quill and pulled it tight.
"If I finish this box," she said, "I will have three to
sell tomorrow. Then Soos is coming with me to see
Mr. Toomis. He may know of a vacant house." She
glanced at him. "Maybe you should come?"

Eli was annoyed. "No. Not me." He thought she had
given in, that she would forget about moving from his
father's house, and he frowned irritably. Catching Nonen's suspicious eyes on him, he turned away and
stood by the door.

"I'll need more quills soon," said Supaya. "Maybe
tomorrow you could get me a porcupine."

"Don't nag me!" exclaimed Eli vehemently. Seeing
the hurt in Supaya's face, he said sarcastically, "Oh
sure. I'll go out and shoot one right out of a tree!"
Supaya bent quickly over her work. After a brief,
strained silence, Eli muttered, "I'm going to Joe's."

Nonen poured Supaya and herself a cup of tea and
sat down opposite her. "You want to move?" she asked,
her wide face solemn.

Supaya heard her disappointment and put aside her
work. "Not because of you," she said earnestly. "You
have been as a mother to me. But . . ." she hesitated,
searching Nonen's face, reluctant in Wenonga's house
to speak his name, ". . . he," emphasizing the word,
"he spies on me. At night. And when you are not
here he . . . comes too close to me."

Nonen understood at once. "It was that way when
my daughter lived here, before she married and moved

into my little hut." She pressed her wide lips together and shook her head. "Eli, he is not strong. . . ."

"When Eli is here, it is better. But I hoped . . . away from his father, in his own house . . . Eli would be . . . happier, more able . . ."

Nonen did not reply to that but drank her tea. After a bit, her face set and threatening, she said, "If he bothers you again, you call me. I am not afraid of him."

The next morning when Supaya spoke to Eli, he mumbled, rolled his head crossly, and refused to open his eyes. Realizing he had been drinking, Supaya pulled the curtain across the door, took her boxes, and walked to the store.

Mrs. Fallon, a trim, neat woman with a small waist, said she would have to call her husband. Her blonde hair, braided in two thick plaits, crossed the top of her head like a coronet. Her queenly manner, pale blue eyes, and almost invisible blonde lashes set her apart from everyone around her, as though she had just stepped out of the fairy-tale illustrations on the large Keen's mustard tins lining the shelves behind her. Like the princess seated on a bank of flowers, encircled by gold scrolls and twining lilies, her face was smooth, delicately tinted, her eyes touched with sweet condescension. She stood aside, then moved to another customer as Jess greeted Supaya and gave his attention to the boxes.

He examined each one, turned it about, removed and replaced the lids. Two were round with the quills arranged in a geometric pattern, the third, round with a leaf design on the lid. "You made these," he said, more statement than question. "I saw your work before, at Mr. Bonnet's." He saw the flicker of surprise in her eyes. "They're beautiful. Fine, distinctive workmanship. If they're for sale, I would like to buy them."

Jess counted the money into her hand. "I'll be happy to buy any others you might make," he added, and giving her a brisk smile, went on to another customer.

Supaya fingered some bolts of cotton print and looked wistfully at a pair of long lisle stockings. But more than she wanted them, she wanted to take all her money home, like a trophy, to prove to Eli what could be done. With the money from the fish, it was a beginning. He would see now how well they could work together.

Eli had just gotten up. "Did you have a good time at Joe's?" asked Supaya. Eli, splashing water over his face and head, mumbled as he rubbed himself with the towel. "Eli, look! I sold the boxes!" Eager for his reaction, she spread the money out on the table.

Nonen clasped her hands and exclaimed with pleasure. Eli raised his eyebrows in comic surprise. "That much for those boxes?"

"Yes, and he said he would buy any more I made! You see how we can manage?" she asked, striving to arouse his cooperation. "With this and the money from the fish, we already have a start." Eli nodded as he casually picked up the money and put it in his pocket. "I'll need more bark and more quills. You'll have to go hunting now."

"Sure," said Eli.

That afternoon Soos went with Supaya to see Mr. Toomis. Like Jackson's, his was a fine stone house with a wide verandah, and the office was in the large front corner room. Mrs. Toomis was not at home, but Gerald, a quiet, red-haired young man, took them hospitably into his office, which, like himself, had a comfortable, easy air. The windows were curtained and a small rug lay in front of the desk. He was sympathetic with Supaya's request for a house, but the only vacant ones were the derelicts she had already seen. If any were vacated, he promised to let her know.

Supaya began at once making more boxes, working in the evenings. Nonen was piecing together sections of old blankets as filling for a quilt. Wenonga, returned from the celebration of his cure, had a fine new blanket hanging from a wall peg and was filling his pipe from a fresh supply of tobacco.

"Abram was looking for you since morning," he said to Eli, who stood by the front door. "He wanted you to fix his harness."

Supaya, whose supply of quills was almost gone, looked up eagerly. "Were you hunting? Did you catch a porcupine?"

"No," said Eli irritably, "I was not hunting!" After a moment he muttered, "I'll go speak to Abram," and left the house.

Out of pride, Supaya went on working, concealing her disappointment. Eli was not responding as she had hoped. He'd been coming home late, and when she proposed fishing again, he'd refused, saying he was not a fisherman and would not go fishing every day.

Wenonga left early the next morning with a purpose of his own, saying nothing to either Nonen or Supaya, who were preparing to make soap. Nonen had already rendered the fat in a large kettle over the outdoor fire when she discovered she had very little lye left.

"Eli can bring us some from the store," said Supaya. Eli was just getting dressed, having slept late again.

"Sure," he said, "I'll get it. Give me some money."

Supaya stared. "Give you . . . what do you mean? You have money."

He brushed past her and went to the wash bench in the lean-to to comb his hair, stooping slightly before the mirror, his elbows angled out. Supaya touched his shoulder. "Eli?"

"I said, give me the money and I'll get the lye!" he exclaimed, exasperated.

"But you have money," insisted Supaya, suddenly alarmed, "all of it! The money for the fish and for the boxes!"

Eli swung round angrily. "I don't have any money!

Why don't you ever listen to what I say! I don't have any money!"

Supaya was stunned. "What happened to it? What did you do with it?"

"A man needs money! I don't have to tell you what I did with it! It's gone, that's all!" His indignation giving him courage, Eli shouted at her. "You're my wife! You have no right to question me!" Then, unable to face her stricken expression, he said self-righteously, "I'm getting out of this house!" He turned to find Nonen blocking the door.

She regarded him scornfully, her eyes cold as Wenonga's. "You disgrace your family," she spat at him, then stepped aside contemptuously, inviting him to go.

Smothering her impulse to cry, Supaya went to Susannah's and borrowed some lye. Together she and Nonen made the soap, pouring the greasy, gray-white mixture into shallow tins which they set in the lean-to to harden. As they worked, Supaya said little, but by the time they finished, her wish to cry had changed to an angry determination to discover what Eli had done with the money.

She went straight to the barn. Nellie was out grazing in the meadow, and the barn, a small building with two stalls, was empty. Supaya began a rapid search, reaching into baskets hung from wall pegs, into the storage bin, into Nellie's manger. There, beneath the fodder, she found an unopened bottle. Behind two bales of hay stacked against the wall, she found another. Wedged between bin and wall, she found a third.

She carried them back to the house and without a word opened them. As Nonen watched, she poured the contents on the ground, and with grim humor, placed the empty bottles in a row by the back door. Then, eyes thoughtfully narrowed, she turned to Nonen, not really seeing her. She was thinking that none of the three bottles had been opened and Eli, when he left, had cut across the meadow toward the woods.

Nonen understood the depth of Supaya's anger and the direction of her thoughts. When Supaya struck off across the meadow, Nonen, seeing her straight back and angry stride, thought of fetching Susannah, but changed her mind. Wenonga would be home soon and she would speak to him.

Supaya headed straight for the bluff. She expected to find Eli there, with an empty bottle, but as she approached, she heard drunken voices, exclamations, and laughter. When she came around the end of the rockfall, she saw a girl, down on her hands and knees, her skirts tumbled forward over her shoulders and head, giggling as Eli, his arms clasped around her middle, his trousers down around his knees, was thrusting himself vigorously against her plump, naked buttocks.

For one moment Supaya stood horrified; then, seized by blind fury, she cried out, and looking for a weapon, saw an empty bottle. Her cry shocked Eli and the girl. Turning, they tumbled over in a heap, Eli rolled sideways, striving to sit up. The girl, struggling with her skirts, saw Supaya smash the bottle against a rock and screamed as Supaya came at them, grasping the jagged bottle like a knife.

Stupified, Eli shrank back against the ground, one arm raised to shield his face as Supaya, wild-eyed, stood above him, her arm on the point of a powerful, downward thrust. The girl was still screaming, waving her arms, frantically trying to ward Supaya off. She was, Supaya suddenly perceived, Marie's friend, Betty.

"You!" Supaya exclaimed, then saw, hanging loosely in the girl's tangled hair, a tortoiseshell comb. Smiling grimly, Supaya commanded, "Take that comb out of your hair!" But the girl continued to scream and flail her arms. Eli half rose, started to speak, but Supaya thrust the bottle at him. "Stay down! You! Take that comb out of your hair!"

This time the girl heard, and with shaking, fumbling fingers drew out the comb.

"Stand up! Stand! Now put that comb on the ground and stomp on it! Harder!"

Eyes rolling with fright, the girl obeyed, frantically stomping the comb into pieces.

"Now go! Fast!" Supaya advanced, jabbing the bottle at her as the girl, screaming at each thrust, retreated. "Don't ever come near him again or you will be sorry! Go! And," she added maliciously, "remember Marie!"

Sobbing, blubbering, the girl turned, fell over a rock, scrambled to her feet and ran.

Eli got up unsteadily, bracing himself against the boulder. His head hung forward, and he stared dully at Supaya from under his brows.

Her initial burst of rage having spent itself, Supaya looked down at the broken bottle and in sudden revulsion threw it from her, far out over the bluff. After a moment, they both heard the faintest shatter of sound.

Eli waited, uncertain what to expect, drained of all initiative. Supaya, in reaction to her violent anger, was overcome by a trembling weakness. Her breathing was hard as if she'd been running. She looked at Eli and saw that he was waiting for her to speak, that he had no strength left, that he was empty. Suddenly, in the bright sunlight, a chill struck her. Shivering, she crossed her arms tightly against herself. She sought to speak to him, and her lips moved, searching for words, but she could find none. Finally, hopelessly, she turned and walked away.

When she had gone, Eli raised his head and looked out over the expanse before him. In the still, limpid air, gulls veered and floated, rising and falling, their wings flashing white against the distant palisade, whose sheer rockface glowed reddish-purple in the strong sunlight. Below, the clear waters of the bay glistened with light, deepening to the rich blue of the lake. Far out was a toylike steamer trailing a tiny banner of smoke.

Overwhelmed by this vast world in which he had no place, bereft of all hope, Eli sank to his knees on the ground. He could not bear what he saw. He could not bear himself. Bending forward, he crossed his arms on the earth before him and rested his head against them, shutting out the light, withdrawing into the darkness of his despair.

Wenonga returned, and seeing the empty bottles standing by the door, needed no explanation from Nonen. Together, they were waiting when Supaya, heartsick and disoriented, came across the meadow. Full of sympathy, Nonen stepped forward to meet her. But Wenonga, with a wide, complacent smile, held out to her two large, plump porcupines.

Supaya stared, then put out her hand and waved them away. She tried to speak, but her throat constricted and tears filled her eyes. She turned her back so they should not see her weakness, but they had seen.

Wenonga laid the porcupines on the ground beside her and went inside. Nonen, her hand on Supaya's shoulder, said softly, "Take them, Suppy, take them."

Sobbing, Supaya shook her head.

But Nonen urged her again. "Take them. They are for you. Pull the quills, and when you finish, I will make us all a fine stew." Then she went inside.

Through tear-blurred eyes, Supaya looked down at the porcupines' limp, spiny bodies. She too was limp, drained of emotion, of anger and of what she now knew was a vain, unreasonable hope. She was done with hoping. Relying solely on her guardian, she would do whatever she had to do, matter-of-factly, and the two porcupines were facts. Sitting down cross-legged,

her back against the lean-to, Supaya began pulling out
quills. She worked calmly, steadily. Her hands were
soon scratched and bleeding, but beside her the pile
of quills grew.

CHAPTER TWELVE

Supaya sat on a log at the edge of the woods, her old shawl pulled close against the chill of a late fall afternoon. Beneath the trees, the earth was layered with leaves, weathered to shiny brown by the autumn rains. She was returning from Soos', where they had slaughtered a pig, and had stopped, as she often did, to sit down and view her fine stone house, Nonen's "little hut." Supaya smiled at Nonen's calling it so because the house was larger than most, with one bedroom downstairs and two up. Besides the usual black iron stove. it had a fireplace like the one in her father's house, and Supaya, from the moment she entered its empty rooms, had felt at home within its stout walls. She and Eli had lived in it for two years now, ever since Nonen's daughter, Mary, and her husband, John, had transferred back to his reserve in the north.

Mary had come one day to Wenonga's house. Stiff with resentment, she made her announcement. She barely touched the tea Nonen poured for her. Her jealousy of Supaya was such that she spoke bluntly to her mother, who seemed to prefer this stranger to herself. "We are leaving the reserve, transferring back to John's reserve."

Nonen was shocked. "Why? You have a home! John is doing well here."

"His mother needs him. She is not well and *she* doesn't want strangers to do for her."

"But my grandchildren!" exclaimed Nonen, dismayed. "When will I ever see them?" She waited, hoping Mary would invite her to come with them.

But Mary said coolly, "It cannot be helped."

Supaya had excused herself and left the room, not wanting to witness Nonen's pain and embarrassment.

Several days later Mary and John had departed, their bed frames, bedding, and a few chairs piled in their wagon. Their small daughter, perched on the bedding, steadied a crate of chickens. Their son dangled his legs over the back and held a rope tied around their cow's neck. As the horse stepped out, the cow bawled in protest and tossed its head at being pulled along at the horse's pace. Nonen stood at the roadside, her hand raised, the children calling, "Good-bye, Grandma!" She watched them until they were out of sight, but her daughter never turned her head.

The next day Nonen had gone to the agent and transferred ownership of her house to Supaya, to be hers now and after Nonen's death.

Before moving in, Supaya and Eli had given the plastered walls and ceiling a fresh coat of whitewash, and he, with an unusual show of vigor and interest, had repaired the broken table legs and built a new bed frame. The shelves had been left on the wall, and with some boards Gerald Toomis gave Supaya, Eli constructed several more and attached them.

Supaya was now thinking that next spring she would enlarge the garden, putting in more potatoes and pumpkins since she got a good price for them at the store. Suddenly it occurred to her that if Eli were to build a small shack with a pen for chickens on one side and a pigpen on the other, she might buy a few chicks and even a shoat in the spring, as Soos had done, to fatten and slaughter in the fall. Since Eli neither hunted nor fished, their meat supply had been scant during the past two winters. Nonen, when she could do so without rousing Wenonga's resentment, had brought them meat and dried fish. But Supaya, knowing how jealously Wenonga guarded his own stores, always tried to give something in return. This year the garden had done well and Supaya was satisfied with what she had laid away in her own root cellar.

A wisp of smoke curled up from the stack. Eli must be home. He had gone with Wenonga to cut wood for their winter fires. She would speak to Eli about building a small barn and pigpen. When he was occupied, he didn't drink so much and seemed more at peace. She had almost reached the house when she heard her name called and saw Nonen running up the lane, her heavy body unwieldy in its blanket but moving fast. Her distress was apparent, and Supaya hurried to meet her.

"You must come!" gasped Nonen. "Sarah fell into the kettle!"

Aghast, Supaya rushed into the house, snatched the velvet medicine bag from her trunk, explained quickly to Eli, and rushed out again, not waiting for Nonen, who followed more slowly.

Before Supaya reached Soos' house, she could hear wailing and screaming. The neighbor's children, who had been racing about, playing with Sarah, had spread news of the accident. Several old women had already arrived and were stooped over Sarah, who was screaming and thrashing about on the ground. Arguing excitedly over what should be done, they were trying awkwardly to remove her clothing. Soos knelt beside her, sobbing hysterically. Behind them steam rose from the huge black kettle set over a pit fire, the scalding water bubbling around the body of the slaughtered pig. Sarah's father, George, and two other men stood helplessly by, somber and tense, watching the women.

"Soos," said Supaya urgently, shaking her shoulder, "bring scissors and a pan of water." Soos, her eyes unfocused, seemed not to comprehend. "Quickly!" Supaya shook her again, and Soos got to her feet, rushed inside, and returned in a moment with scissors and a basin. The old women stood back, weeping and wailing, as Supaya deftly cut away Sarah's clothes. Using roots and leaves from her medicine bag, Supaya combined some root of the swamp tea plant, *kinnikinnick* leaves, white poplar root, and balm-of-Gilead poplar root, pounded to a pulp, and added enough water to make a strong infusion. Speaking calmly to Sarah, Supaya gently rolled her over and bathed her neck and back with the solution. As she did so, a large section of hair and scalp came off in her hand, exposing the raw, red back of Sarah's head. Soos gasped and fell forward, hiding her face against her knees; the wailing of the women increased in volume. Working rapidly, Supaya ordered Soos to make a bed of cedar boughs in the house and cover it with a clean quilt. More women had arrived and stood about crying and wringing their hands. Others silently watched or helped Supaya by holding Sarah's head and arms as she bathed the burns. Sarah had tripped and fallen backwards into the kettle. Luckily, the pig's body had kept her head from going under, and one of the men, hearing her screams, had grabbed her legs in time to keep the lower part of her body from falling into the scalding water.

When the pallet was ready, Supaya and an old woman carried Sarah inside and laid her face down, her head turned to one side. All the old women filed inside after them and lined up around the walls of the room, their lamentation rising like a chorus. One sank down on her knees and rocked back and forth, her shawl shading her face, keening in a low, sorrowful voice.

Supaya cut short Sarah's remaining hair and gave it to Soos, who put it in a bag with the rest for George to bury. Then Supaya mixed dried lady slipper root in a cup and coaxed Sarah to swallow it, pouring a little at a time into her mouth and massaging her throat to

induce her to swallow. "Now cover her just to her
waist. I will be back soon."

In a nearby field Supaya gathered plantain leaves.
With these she made a warm, wet poultice and spread
it over the burned areas. Soos sat on the floor beside
the bed, her eyes red, her face strained with fear.

"She will sleep now," said Supaya. She laid her hand
comfortingly on Soos' arm. "She will be all right. I'll
come back soon and stay with her."

When Supaya returned in the early evening, she
brought a jug containing a solution made from the
soft inner bark of the basswood tree. Sarah had wak-
ened and was whimpering. Speaking softly to her, Supaya bathed the burns, applied a fresh poultice, and
again gave her a sleeping potion.

The old women were still there, now silent specta-
tors. Some had gone and returned with food for Susannah and George. The woman who had been keening, Sarah's grandmother, sat against the wall, her
face shadowed by her shawl, but her eyes gleamed in
the lamplight, alert to all that Supaya did. Soos, five
months pregnant, gripped her hands nervously together, and George stood close beside, his face grim.

Using her sleeping powder, Supaya made them both
a hot drink. "You must get some sleep," she told Soos.
"This will help you. Now go, both of you. I'll stay with
Sarah." As at a signal, all the old women silently filed
out of the house. Supaya turned the lamp low and
pulled Soos' rocking chair close to Sarah's pallet. Now
and then Supaya dozed, but several times during the
night, without waking the child, she bathed the burns
and renewed the poultice.

The next day the old women returned, taking a deep
interest in Sarah's condition and Supaya's treatment.
With Susannah and George, still anxious but composed, they watched as Supaya bathed the burns, now
turning a dark reddish purple, and put on a fresh
poultice. They could see that her curing was good and

complimented Supaya indirectly by making quiet, re-assuring comments to the parents.

That night also Supaya stayed and then came to treat Sarah each day until the healing had progressed well enough for Soos to care for her.

News of Sarah's curing spread rapidly. At church, women who had ignored Supaya as an outsider and kept their distance because she was Wenonga's daughter-in-law now spoke to her politely, indicating their willingness to accept her. Supaya returned their greetings with equal politeness, but sat, proud and dignified, where she always sat, in the back row with Soos, and made no effort to cultivate their friendship.

Supaya had begun attending church partly to please Susannah, who wanted her company, and partly to please Mrs. Crowell. Shortly after Supaya had moved into Nonen's "little hut," Amy Crowell had appeared at Supaya's door, looking as surprised to find herself there as if she had arrived accidentally. She held a potted plant against her chest and stood half turned from the door, ready to hurry off at the first alarm. When Supaya opened the door, she smiled and stepped back as though her presence were an embarrassment to them both.

Supaya, truly pleased to see her, put out both hands and drew her inside. "Welcome! Welcome! Please come in. I am happy you have come." She indicated one of the two straight chairs Nonen had loaned them. "Please sit down. We will have a cup of tea."

Amy Crowell sat. She had not been inside an Indian home since coming to the reserve, and she gazed about with childlike curiosity at the bumpy, whitewashed walls and dark ceiling beams, at the clothes hanging on pegs and the bare, wooden floor. There were no curtains at the small windows and few dishes on the shelves. But there were large, colorful tins of cornstarch, tea, and baking powder, decorated with scenes from Aesop's Fables and portraits of Queen

Victoria, all in soft, muted shades of blue, brown, red, and gold. And on a shelf near the fireplace were books, several that had belonged to Supaya's mother as well as her own, including a composition book in which she recorded sales of baskets, mats, and vegetables.

"Why," said Amy, "we have cottages like this at home in England!" She settled back in her chair, then remembered she was still holding the pot. "Here, my dear, I wanted to bring you this. Reverend Crowell is making calls this morning, you see, and dropped me off here. He thinks I don't get out enough. He always wants me to go calling with him, but I . . . ," she paused, looking flustered, ". . . you understand what it is to be a stranger, and . . . but I wanted to come to see you! He doesn't know that," she added, her pale eyes suddenly sly, as if she had played a trick on her unsuspecting husband. "I wanted you to have this. I raised it from seeds from my home in England. It's fine for borders. Of course . . ." she hesitated, perplexed, "no one plants borders here. But you could . . . could . . . ," she broke off helplessly, at a loss to say what Supaya could do.

Supaya turned the pot about admiringly. "I will start a border. I'll plant it beside the front door." Gently she touched the drooping leaves and fragile blossoms. "It's very pretty, and it's kind of you to give me a flower from your home. It will always be special to me."

Reassured, Amy happily drank her tea.

A few days later Amy came again. This time she carried several rolls of wallpaper. Eli was home, putting an ash splint seat in a chair he had made. Unused to his presence, Amy stood back shyly while Supaya unrolled the paper, a few leftover pieces from Amy's living room, patterned with red roses and twining green leaves.

"Eli, look!" Supaya exclaimed. "It's so pretty!"

Embarrassed by their gratitude, Amy tried to explain her gift. "You admired it, so I wanted you to have it. I thought . . . you could use it . . . that is, it's not enough to . . ." Suddenly realizing that what she had brought was insufficient to cover even one wall of the room, her eyes darted about in dismay. "Maybe . . ." she appealed to Supaya, ". . . maybe you could . . ."

"I will line the backs of the shelves with it," said Supaya confidently, and Amy, rescued, smiled with relief.

She was curious about what Eli was doing, and he kindly explained, showing her as he would a child how he wove the splints. He believed, as did all the Indians, that Amy was not like other people. In a world where evil was always mixed with good, she had been blessed with total innocence. Her fragile spirit was naturally confused. Because she could never be at ease, she must be treated tenderly. Reverend Crowell, absorbed in his work and unaware of the special light in which his wife was viewed, would have been surprised to know to what extent the faithful attendance and cooperation of his flock was due to their care for his wife.

Lizzie Toomis had also come to call when Supaya moved into her own house, announcing herself by a loud, forceful knock. Energetic and at home wherever she went, Lizzie took a frank, lively interest in Supaya's house, and recognized immediately Amy's wallpaper. "How clever of you to use it that way," she remarked, accepting a cup of tea. "But you need curtains, don't you? I'll look in my trunk when I get home and see if I have anything suitable." She brought Supaya a china teapot, white, with sprays of pale pink flowers. "I thought you'd like a teapot," she said firmly, having never doubted it.

Supaya responded to this forthright young woman and expressed her delight with the teapot, admiring the gold-edged spout and twisted gold handle on the lid. It was her first piece of china, and she placed it prominently in the middle of a shelf.

Lizzie did look in her trunk and found two pairs of curtains, which Supaya hung at the living room windows. Remembering how Wenonga had watched her through the window, Supaya now slept upstairs in the front bedroom.

Wenonga had not come to her house, and Supaya saw him less often now. Occasionally Soos, lowering her voice as if Wenonga could hear her no matter where she was, whispered gossip about him, how he had left one man's wife and pursued another's, who had been compelled to give in to him for fear of what he might do to her family.

Supaya was never quite sure when she first saw the white dog. She often took a shortcut through the woods to Soos' and several times had caught a fleeting glimpse of a white shape slipping through the brush, or the sun glancing off the white back of a dog disappearing through the trees. She thought little of it.

But one morning on her way to the store, she rounded a bend and there he was, standing by a tree, his eyes fixed expectantly on her as if he'd known she was coming. Supaya stopped dead. He was huge, and his size, the richness of his fur that fanned out in a thick ruff about his ears and neck, the extraordinary expression in his eyes, as if he could speak if he chose, the sense of power that emanated from him, all made clear that he was to be feared. Now Supaya understood her mistake in thinking past glimpses of him had been mere chance. She felt his strength projected powerfully against her, willing her, compelling her to falter, to retreat. Almost imperceptibly he extended his neck and lowered his head, never taking his eyes from hers. Bracing herself, Supaya faced him unwaveringly, trying to mask the deep fear she felt of so deadly an antagonist. But she knew she must do more than just withstand him. She must move first. Remembering the stone bear in her pouch, she addressed it silently, "Grandfather, help me! Give me courage!" And forcing herself to move, she took a bold, challenging step forward. Watching her with shining eyes and one paw slightly lifted, the great dog hesitated briefly. Then, tossing his head in a playful motion, he leaped aside and bounded away into the woods. Supaya did not look after him, making herself walk on, as though unconcerned. But she drew a deep, shuddering breath and her shoulders were limp with relief.

At the store, Jess Fallon came to greet her as he always did, smiling and pleased to see her. "Good morning, Mrs. Red Sky. How are you today?" He laid his hands flat on the counter and leaned slightly forward.

"I am well, thank you." Her voice sounded stiff and unnatural in her own ears, but Supaya was always confused by Jess Fallon. The sparkle in his blue eyes made her unaccountably blush, as the look of no other man ever did. Feeling her face grow warm, she would hold her head all the higher, trying to be dignified. But then she suspected him of being amused, and because she was never certain of whether he was teasing her or not, her voice, to her chagrin, would almost die away.

She had brought more boxes to sell. He examined them, commenting so anyone could hear. Supaya, pleased by his praise but aslo embarrassed, sensing the notice taken of her by others in the store, made a slight, impatient gesture.

Perceiving her embarrassment, Jess put the boxes aside and paid her, one dollar per box, "You know," he said, "you could make more money and with less work and time." Surprised, Supaya looked directly at him, her eyes wide and questioning. "You could make splint baskets. See, like these." He pointed to a low shelf behind the counter where ash splint baskets of various sizes were stacked. "They sell very well. I could pay fifty cents for the apple and lunch baskets, seventy-five for the clothes hamper, maybe more for a good sewing basket."

Immediately Supaya saw the possibilities and began wondering how she could get some splints. Maybe Eli could . . .

Watching her, Jess saw her eagerness and speculation. "Just a minute." He went into a small storage room and returned with a bundle of splints. "Old Joe traded me these the other day. Why don't you start with them." Supaya drew back, unwilling to accept any favors. "Go on. Take them. I'll deduct the price from the baskets when you bring them in." Still she hesitated, looking at him doubtfully. "I mean it. See, I'll make a note of the amount." He scribbled some words and figures on a pad by the cash drawer and then smiled, as if inviting her to share in a joke.

Uncertain whether she was being teased or not, Supaya, her cheeks a dusky pink, took the bundle of splints and said primly, "Thank you. I will remember."

On the way home she kept to the main road and was alert for any movement or rustle in the underbrush, and was particularly watchful at the bend in the road, but the white dog didn't appear.

She put away her money in a box that also held Quayo's glowing powder. She had kept it there ever since the day she had surprised Eli with money in his hand and the can she had hidden it in empty on the table. She had told him to put it back.

Eli, startled, then angry and defensive, had yelled, "I am the man in this house! I take what I want! It is mine by right!"

"It is not yours to waste on drink! Or," seeing his slight sneer, "to buy fancy combs for your women! That is not a man's way! A real man would not soil himself or his family!"

He grinned at her and kept the money in his fist. "I was man enough for you! But you have given me no family! Others have. Maybe it is you who are no good as a woman!"

Cold with anger but, like her father, deceptively quiet, she said only, "Put it back, Eli."

"No," he answered rashly, thinking that settled the matter, and turned to go.

With catlike swiftness, Supaya snatched up the hatchet from beside the stove and came at him, holding the gleaming, knife-sharp edge at an angle before her. "Put it back," she repeated, her lips scarcely moving, her eyes narrowed with purpose. Her hand gripping the haft, she moved the blade slightly back and forth.

Stunned, Eli stared at the blade, then, as she moved deliberately closer, he saw the deadly intent in her face. After the briefest hesitation, he laid the money down.

Still holding the hatchet, Supaya got Quayo's little box of powder. As she opened it, Eli shrank back. "Now," said Supaya coldly, "I will no longer hide the money. It will be here, with this box, and you, the man of the house," with scornful emphasis, "will always know where it is."

Suddenly, Eli backed still further off, then intimidated and unable to bear her contempt, he fled from the house.

All during the fall and into winter Supaya worked on splint baskets. When Soos and George saw what she was doing, George, feeling deeply obligated for Sarah's healing, offered to cut the ash when spring came and pound it into splints, thus keeping her well supplied.

Soos had her baby, another girl, and to relieve her, Supaya often took Sarah for the day. There was strong affection between them. As Supaya worked, Sarah learned by imitation to make her own little baskets from scraps and pieces. Her burns were now healed, and her hair had grown back, thick but still short, giving her a pert and saucy look. Supaya promised to help her make her own lunch basket for school and her own sewing basket.

One chill, gray afternoon when snow clouds rolled in low and threatening, Supaya and Sarah sat at the table working. Supaya was finishing a long, narrow bread basket designed to hold eight loaves in a row for the lady shoppers in Wellston. Sarah was painstakingly weaving natural and brown splints into a basket as a present for her mother. The teakettle simmered on the stove, and bannock, a treat for Sarah, filled the room with its aroma. Supaya glanced up in time to catch sight through the window of a wagon pulling up before the house. When she opened the door, Jess Fallon stood on her doorstep, holding his black, wide-brimmed hat in his hand and smiling.

"Afternoon, Mrs. Red Sky. I'm pleased to find you home."

Supaya, finding her voice, said, "Welcome to my home. Please come in."

Sarah, abandoning her work at sight of him, smiled broadly, her head coyly to one side, waiting for him to notice her.

"Why, there's Miss Sarah," he exclaimed, and catching her under her arms, swung her up and down again. Sarah kicked her feet and laughed with pleasure. She liked this big man who slipped her cookies when she came to his store with her mother.

"Please sit down," said Supaya, grateful for Sarah's presence. "We will have some tea."

"Thank you. I'd appreciate that. It's a chilly day." He sat down, very much at ease, filling the room with his presence and looking not at all chilled. "But it's very cozy in here, isn't it, Sarah." He reached in his coat pocket and drew out an envelope. "A letter came for you, Mrs. Red Sky. As I was passing, I thought I'd drop it off."

Supaya turned instantly. The envelope was small

and thin. The writing she recognized as Jacques'. Restraining her eagerness to read it, she poured tea and brought the bannock to the table.

"Go ahead, read it. Sarah and I won't mind, will we?" Sarah, totally engrossed by Jess, leaned against his knee and gazed at him with big, shining eyes. Her mouth full of bread, she shook her head in agreement as if mesmerized.

The letter was brief. Jacques and Maud were married and living in Auntie Em's house. She had died last spring and had left her house to Quayo, who had given it to them. Neegonas was going to have another baby. Joe Crow had died. They had found him one morning lying by the fireplace.

Reading the letter, like hearing unexpectedly the voice of a loved one, made Supaya suddenly long for home. She could not bear to know that Auntie Em had died or Joe Crow, or that anything had changed at all since she left. Silently she folded the letter and put it away.

Though she kept her head bent, Jess saw that her lip trembled. Suppressing an impulse to take her hands and comfort her, he tried to divert her. "This is fine bread, isn't it, Sarah. I think you need another piece. And if that pot has a bit more tea in it . . ." He held out his cup, and Supaya, recalled by the demands of hospitality, hastened to refill it. He examined the baskets Supaya and Sarah had been working on. He praised Sarah's and, to her delight, asked that she make him one just like it. Taking up the bread basket, he admired Supaya's geometric variation on the usual checkerboard pattern.

Her attention finally caught, Supaya looked critically at the long basket. "Do you have any dyes?" she asked, "white man's dyes, red or green? Maybe yellow?"

He pondered. "I may have." He saw that in discussing the baskets and dyes, she had spoken to him more naturally, as to a friend, and he added quietly so as not to break her mood, "If not, I can get some next time I go to Wellston."

"Red or green would be prettier, brighter than brown. Or," putting her head to one side, "I could combine them. And I wondered about lining the sewing baskets with cotton print. What do you think? Would that make them sell better?" She turned to him suddenly and caught in his eyes a dreamy, gentle warmth as they rested on her, a look so preoccupied he seemed not to have heard a word she'd said. But as she paused in surprise, his expression altered so swiftly she thought what she'd seen a mere trick of the fading winter light. He answered at once, in a businesslike tone.

Sarah, fascinated by his gold watch chain, extended one stubby finger toward it, and he had just taken out his pocket watch and held it to her ear when Eli entered through the back door.

Seeing the three of them, he stopped short and stood stiffly by the stove. He nodded his head once in response to Jess' greeting and refused the tea and bread Supaya offered him. He had been gone several days. His clothes were dirty, his hair uncombed. Heavy-eyed, he stared antagonistically at the elegant white man sitting at his table.

"Well," said Jess, "I must go. Thank you for the tea, Mrs. Red Sky. I'll see if I can get those dyes." Sarah followed him to the door and waved as he turned the wagon smartly and held up his hat in salute.

"What was he doing here?" asked Eli sullenly. "Come to see my wife?"

Angry that she had to feel ashamed of her husband, Supaya said coldly, "He stopped to bring me a letter from home. My brother is married, and my Auntie Em died."

Eli, immediately losing interest, went into his own bedroom and pulled the curtain.

Snow had come early that year, and the winter was long and bitter. Many had severe colds or developed pneumonia. Having witnessed Supaya's skill in healing, women began coming to her for cures. They had known her father was a shaman, but now, impressed by her own ability as an herbalist, they appealed readily to her for help. Otherwise they kept a respectful distance. Though she lived apart in her own house, she was still Wenonga's daughter-in-law, and aside from Soos and George, her friends were white. Increasingly, Supaya spent more time preparing medicines and walking from house to house, visiting patients all over the reserve. Sometimes, if she were to be late, Eli accompanied her until he developed a cough, which he seemed unable to get rid of and impatiently refused to let her treat.

Always she watched for the white dog, whose huge paw prints she occasionally found outside the house in the early morning. One moonlit night, looking out from her upstairs window across the pale, glittering snow, she saw him, luminous white against white, standing on his own oblique black shadow. Slowly he raised his head and stared upward. Though she stood in the dark, she felt that his eyes, struck by the moonlight, looked straight at her. Suddenly he turned and ran off, his shadow gliding smoothly beside him over the snow.

In return for her healing, she was paid by gifts of food, and so she and Eli fared better that winter than in previous winters. She made and sold many baskets. Jess stocked the dyes she asked for, and once he brought back from Wellston a large bundle of cotton print remnants.

"For lining the baskets," he said, showing them to her.

Supaya wanted to buy them; some pieces were even

large enough for a blouse or a summer dress for Sarah. "But not today," said Supaya, thinking of the flour and tea she had to buy, as well as the dyes.

"Take them," said Jess. "They're free."

"Free!" Supaya exclaimed, looking at him in disbelief.

"I got them for nothing. Only had to carry them back." Innocently, he raised his eyebrows at her. "The warehouse was throwing them away." Seeing her disbelief, he added guilelessly, "They're a wasteful people."

Supaya smiled slightly. "Then I will pay you for your trouble."

He appeared to calculate, then said, solemnly, "I figure it at fifteen cents."

Equally solemn, but suddenly shy and pink-cheeked, Supaya carefully counted out the money.

In early January the chief held his annual feast in the Council Hall for all members of the band. For three days all the women of his family busied themselves preparing food. Supaya was up unusually early because she had promised Soos, the chief's third daughter, to help set tables and serve food. She stepped outside to a pearly gray morning. But to the east, above the trees, a red glow was spreading across the sky, casting a rosy light on the snow. Wrapped in a blanket, Supaya walked along the road between drifts as high as the fence posts. Her breath hung like smoke in the dry, still air. Far off, she heard the cawing of a crow, its voice clear and resonant. Gradually it came nearer, and she saw it, black against the sky, a long crow soaring and circling. When she entered Soos' back door, the warm air making her face tingle, she could still hear its call.

The feast was attended by everyone living on the reserve. Grandly the chief received them all, making them welcome and inviting them to sit and eat. Supaya ran back and forth all day, helping Soos, her mother, sisters, aunts, and cousins serve the guests and keep the platters and bowls full for each successive group. When all had been fed and were listening to speeches and singing songs, Supaya, feeling weary, whispered to Soos that she was leaving early.

There had been no wind all day. The light was fading as quietly as it had come. The snow, packed down by wagon wheels, squeaked faintly underfoot. She was nearly home when suddenly, with a clap of wings, a crow swooped past her, skimming low. He veered from side to side across the road ahead, then landed and folded back his wings. Cocking his eye at Supaya, he strutted ahead of her, thrusting his head forward to utter short, rasping squawks. Astonished, Supaya saw that he pitched to one side. Like Joe Crow, he had one injured leg. Drawn to him, she moved closer. With a heavy flap of his wings, he rose in the evening air and soared ahead, landing on the ridge of her roof. Loath to lose sight of him, Supaya ran after him and stood with arm outstretched, clucking at him, hoping to coax him down. But he only cocked his head and stepped restlessly back and forth, turning in little circles. When only a narrow ribbon of deep red showed on the western horizon below the darkened sky, he took off again, with a heavy beat of his wings, into the last light.

With a pang as if a heartstring had snapped, Supaya looked after him until he was only a black speck against the dying day and then vanished altogether.

That night she slept fitfully, starting awake from confused and frightening dreams. Toward morning she fell into a deep sleep, awakening later than usual, with only one clear memory: her father, his face shadowed, speaking her name.

She dressed and made up the fire. When Eli came home, yawning, she was standing by the window gazing out at the snowdrifts, wishing with a deep sense of urgency that winter would soon be over. She resolved that when the lake ice split in the spring, she would go home.

CHAPTER THIRTEEN

No one knew she was coming, for there was no way a letter could arrive before she did. Nor had she spoken of her intention—not even to Nonen or Soos. Her request, put to George, to be taken into Wellston had surprised them all. Only Jess Fallon had known, since she'd depended on him to tell her the first sailing date.

Six years had passed since her arrival in Wellston. Supaya was no longer an inexperienced girl of sixteen to be frightened by a town that was smaller and dirtier than she'd remembered, or by strange people, Indian or white. Calm and composed, she boarded the steamer, choosing, this trip, to sit inside the cabin. Other passengers, carrying odd assortments of bags and bundles, entered, letting in cold gusts of air. Proximity and the exhilaration of beginning a journey together made them convivial, and they struck up small conversations. But Supaya sat apart, her face turned to the window.

She watched as the steamer plowed its way through the dark, cold water, ice floes swirling aside from its prow. At each stop along the way, freight was loaded and unloaded, mailbags exchanged for other mailbags, and passengers, clutching their belongings, hurried down the gangway past others who were hurrying up. Supaya took little notice. Only once, later in the afternoon, when the stopover seemed unusually long, did she rise impatiently and walk about the now nearly empty cabin. The sky, overcast when they left Wellston, was clearing. Long rifts appeared in the ragged, cottony clouds, revealing a bright blue above, and through those rifts sunlight shone down in hazy columns that glittered on the distant ice. Becoming aware of her own reflection in the glass, Supaya wondered uneasily now that the time was almost come—Stone Island was the next stop—how her father would greet her. Concern for him, a deep conviction that something was wrong and her help was needed, had made her determined to come. But the reality of their meeting had not struck her until this moment, as she faced her own dim, transparent image.

She had parted from him without a word, leaving behind, like a slap in his face, the most treasured gift he had to give her. She longed to see her home again, and her grandmother and brother, but most of all her father, to restore the harmony between them. Like a repentant child she wanted him to know that time had brought her some understanding, that she had long since seen he'd had no choice. Of Kineu, she dared not think.

Raising her shawl over her head, Supaya went out on deck. The wind blew hard. It whipped her skirts and caught her breath. But she held her shawl across her mouth, braced herself against the rail and stared intently ahead, over the choppy water.

Gradually Stone Island appeared, rising out of the lake. To the west the lowering sun glanced across the surface of the water, setting off millions of shifting, sparkling lights and illuminating the island in a soft, warm glow. A dream island, it floated above the water, its bare, rocky peak clear against the fragile evening sky. Supaya's memory, like a soaring bird, looked down from a height upon the summit, at the hollow hidden among the rocks, where she had lifted her arms to the Great Spirit and been blessed with a vision.

Startled by the steamer's whistle, its vibrations carried away by the wind, she saw they were passing

Auntie Em's house, where she and Kineu had made love in the loft as Auntie Em had rocked in her chair, smiling and eating Quayo's berry pie. Now Auntie Em was dead, and the boy and girl that Supaya and Kineu had been no longer existed. Now Jacques and Maud lived there and the shadows of others had faded away even as the smoke from Maud's fire thinned and faded into the air.

The steamer rounded a point of land and the end of the wharf came forward to meet them, chunks of ice nudging its weathered piers. On the rocky beach lay a few small boats, hulls up. Beyond the wharf and an open stretch of ground was the general store, all just as before except that everything had shrunk. The wharf was flimsy and narrow. The ground beyond was not the wide space she remembered. The store, bleached as a dead tree, looked absurdly small, and its porch roof sagged in the middle. Responding to the ship's repeated whistle, several figures detached themselves from the porch and moved toward the wharf. Behind them a man in shirt sleeves hurried down the steps, braving the chill wind that whipped his apron. He waved his arms and called out, striving comically to make himself heard. Supaya smiled to herself: Mr. Bonnet, ordering people about. That, at least, was the same. Carrying her bag and basket, she stepped down the gangplank and walked toward him, thinking with amusement how different he'd find it if he tried to bargain with her now. As she passed, he paused in his shouting long enough to nod politely at an attractive stranger. A second later, arms still raised, he turned in surprise, to stare after her.

Supaya walked on, having no time to waste on Mr. Bonnet. She did not hurry in her white woman's shoes, stepping carefully to avoid muddy, water-filled ruts. The time of year was the same as when she had left— trees just coming into leaf, gray-brown fields sodden with melted snow. But only the time was the same.

The circumstances were entirely different. She had come only because she herself had resolved to come. She had paid for her passage and the gifts she brought with money she herself had earned. She had come when she chose and she would leave when she chose. Only planting time limited her freedom. No longer did anyone—certainly not Eli—presume to order her about, and she smiled to think how proud her father and grandmother would be of her independence.

She passed the agent's house, stone, like hers, but its porch columns badly in need of paint after a hard winter, and further on, the schoolhouse, its windows glassily reflecting the fading sunset. Near the crossroads stood the preacher's house, already shadowed by the growing dusk under the fir trees. Beyond was the stone church, light still touching its narrow bell tower, and the cemetery, where her mother had long been buried and where in a cold November they had buried Aunt Theresa and this past winter, Auntie Em.

Turning off onto a smaller road, Supaya saw a man walking toward her. She caught her breath in sudden panic. Could it be Kineu? The twilight was deceptive, and his straight-brimmed black hat shaded his face. She had not expected to meet him like this, in the middle of a road! She tried to maintain her composure, but her feet, carrying her forward of their own accord, stumbled, and like a fool she soaked her shoes and splashed her skirt with mud. The man came steadily on. Feeling quite faint, she forced herself to look at him as they passed each other, then closed her eyes for an instant, limp with relief. He was not Kineu! He was no one she knew. But eager now to have the moment of meeting over, she hurried on and reached her father's doorstep as twilight was deepening into night.

She knocked and at once a cry came from within as if she had struck the living bones of the house. She waited, wanting to smile, fighting an impulse to cry.

She heard voices arguing; then the door jerked open and Rhea, her hair disheveled, confronted her belligerently. The lamplight fell on Supaya, and from within the room a tremulous voice cried:

"Come! Supaya, come!"

Astonished, Rhea stepped back as Supaya rushed past her and embraced her grandmother, sitting in her rocker by the fireplace.

"Ah! Ah! I knew you were coming! I knew!" Quayo, her face alight, leaned her gray head against Supaya's and clasped her with arms still strong and wiry. "Let me look at you." She held Supaya's shoulders and studied her. It was then that Supaya saw that Quayo's eyes, once shiny-black as a bird's, were cloudy gray. "Ah," said Quayo, touching Supaya's face, "you have learned much. You have climbed a long way."

Supaya, choking back her tears, whispered, "It is good to see you, Grandmother! It is good to be home!"

Smiling, Quayo leaned back in her chair and said, "Rhea, some tea. My granddaughter has come home."

Supaya rose, and turning, saw her father standing in his bedroom doorway. The sight of him struck her heart like a blow. He, who always stood so proudly erect, whose jaunty, swaggering step caught every woman's eye, now stood bent over, shoulders hunched, his head thrust forward at an angle. His hair hung about his face, straggly and uncombed.

"Father!" Supaya could not hide her dismay. She reached for his hand, but his fingers were stiff and curled like a dead bird's claw, and she could only cradle it in her own.

With a wry smile that hid the shame he felt at her seeing him so, Jules said, "Welcome home, Daughter. Our hearts rejoice to see you. Come, we will sit down and speak together. You must have much to tell us."

That night Supaya was glad to climb the steps to her old bed in the loft. She needed rest and time alone with her thoughts. She knew now she'd been foolish for doubting her father would welcome her, and was ashamed for having so misjudged him. And she had been right to come. Another year would have been too late. Jacques and Maud came to help them, but otherwise they were left to themselves, except, as her father contemptuously remarked, for Reverend Harris, who came too often, demanding that Jules marry Rhea in the church. Supaya understood why they were shunned. The three of them, like the house, were dirty and unkempt. The air stank of unwashed bodies, dirty clothes, and pots. How it must grieve Quayo, always proud of her appearance and her home, and Jules, proud of his skill as a healer and prowess as a hunter, now crippled so he could no longer heal, or hunt, or fish. Visitors would not be comfortable with such a distressing host or in such an oppressive, caustic atmosphere. Whose secret envy or resentment could have brought this evil on them? Whoever it was, whatever the cause, she would need all her blessings to cure it.

As they had drunk their tea, Jules, obviously in pain, had listened attentively as she'd told them of her new life, hearing what she said and what she did not say. Rhea sat apart, like an outsider, nursing her resentments. Supaya was conscious of her envious eyes studying her hair, her clothes and shoes.

Supaya said nothing of her stillbirth, but spoke warmly of Nonen and the fine stone house she'd given her. She told them of Soos and her white friends, Amy and Lizzie, and of her rapidly increasing work as a healer. Jules saw then that his daughter was respected but set apart by her own people. And Supaya told about the kinds of baskets she made and the white man who helped supply her with materials and who bought her vegetables and baskets. Jules' sharp ears heard the subtle change in her voice when she spoke